'You really are something special, Miss Leila Thomas.'

She didn't answer Blaize's smile. She disliked him far too much for that. Her voice was dry. 'Resources have to be managed, Mr Oliver, including human resources. I don't have to teach you that, surely? As an extremely efficient secretary, which is what I am, I can be of some value to you. As a bit of slap and tickle beside the pool, I would be totally wasted. I'm sure there are lots of women perfectly eager and willing to fill that role for you.'

'But supposing I like mixing my business with my pleasure?' he smiled, drawing one finger gently down the nape of her neck in a way that awoke goose-bumps across her spine.

Books you will enjoy
by MADELEINE KER

A SPECIAL ARRANGEMENT

It might be the twentieth century, but arranged
marriages still existed, as Romy found out when
Xavier de Luca blackmailed her into marrying
him. He wanted heirs for his Sicilian estate, and
in return he would save Romy's father from
bankruptcy. But could she cope with such an
arrangement when her feelings for him were so
extreme?

PASSION'S FAR SHORE

Dorothy had accepted the job as governess to
Pearl, not because she wanted to go to Japan,
but because the little girl needed her. But it
seemed Pearl's father, Calum Hescott, thought
differently...

TIGER'S EYE

BY

MADELEINE KER

MILLS & BOON LIMITED
ETON HOUSE   18-24 PARADISE ROAD
RICHMOND   SURREY   TW9 1SR

*First published in Great Britain 1989
by Mills & Boon Limited*

© Madeleine Ker 1989

*Australian copyright 1989
Philippine copyright 1990
This edition 1990*

ISBN 0 263 76560 1

*Set in Times Roman 10 on 11 pt.
01-9002-58057 C*

Made and printed in Great Britain

CHAPTER ONE

Leila pushed her suitcases through the Customs area unchallenged, and emerged into the balmy warmth of the main airport hall.

There were several signs being held up among the crowd of people awaiting Flight BA 304 from London, and it took her a moment to locate the one that was for her. It read 'CLAREWELL'. Not her own name, nor that of her future employer, but the name of the London agency that had sent her.

She gave the girl holding it a quick wave, and wheeled her trolley round the railings.

'Hi,' Leila greeted her with a smile. 'I'm Leila Thomas.'

'Hello,' came the cool greeting back. A pair of green eyes looked her up and down with not very friendly interest. 'Got all your luggage?'

'This is it.'

'Come on, then. I've left the car outside, and you're not meant to do that.'

Without further ado, she led the way to the nearest exit, giving Leila a chance to assess very pretty legs and a mass of glossy chestnut hair.

It was even hotter outside. The skies over Barcelona were a deep, almost violet blue, and there wasn't a hint of cloud. Palm trees rustled in the barest of breezes— just enough to tell Leila that her skin was already damp with the heat.

'Whew!' she commented brightly. 'This is hotter than I expected!'

'If you expected it to be cool in July, you obviously don't know the Costa Brava.'

'I've never been to Spain before,' Leila confessed.

'It's hot,' the girl said succinctly. She opened the boot of the car, an all-white Volkswagen Golf convertible, and stood waiting for Leila to load her own luggage, obviously not intending to help.

Leila hefted the lighter cases in first, then finished off with the heaviest one, gasping a little with the effort.

'What have you got in there?' she was asked scornfully. 'Fur coats?'

'Not exactly,' Leila replied, straightening. She glanced at the other girl for a moment. She was very pretty, with quite startlingly beautiful green eyes and petite, rather snub features. The rounded, bee-stung mouth looked both sulky and spoiled, though whether that was a permanent state, or due to some temporary irritation, there was no way of telling. Her figure was small, but with feminine curves in all the right places. Her breasts pushed aggressively against the silk blouse.

Despite all that, Leila now saw that she was very young—not more than eighteen. 'Are you a member of Mr Oliver's staff?' she asked politely.

'Hell, no. I'm Mr Oliver's daughter,' came the disdainful reply.

'Oh.' She still hadn't bothered to give Leila a first name, so Leila decided that 'Miss Oliver' was evidently what was expected from menials. 'Well, thank you for meeting me, Miss Oliver.'

'You'd never have found the place on your own.' Miss Oliver slammed the boot shut with a thump, and nodded Leila to the passenger door. 'Let's go.'

The inside of the car was all white leather, and smelled strongly of Miss Oliver's rather heavy perfume. Miss Oliver checked her reflection in the rear-view mirror, taking a moment to brush some dust off the eyelashes which were heavily coated with mascara. Her scarlet nails were a little overlong for the job, however, and she grimaced, muttering.

Then she started the Golf, crashed into gear, and set off with a squeal of tyres, weaving in and out of the more sedate traffic around them.

Leila clung to the strap beside her. Her companion's awful driving was made all the more hair-raising by the fact that she only had one hand on the wheel. The other was scrabbling in the glove compartment for a cassette tape. She located the one she wanted, and slotted it into the complex-looking car stereo.

A crashing blast of up-to-the-minute heavy rock invaded the car, making Leila wince. Miss Oliver's dainty pink ears were evidently less sensitive, however, because she was nodding in satisfaction to the beat. She popped a sliver of chewing-gum into her sulky mouth, put her hand—much to Leila's relief—back on the wheel, and settled down to driving with quite dramatic badness down the *autopista* towards Barcelona.

She made no other effort to talk to Leila, and the ear-splitting music made any conversational gambits on her own part futile, so Leila just looked out of the window at the skyline of Barcelona. You met all sorts as a temporary secretary. She had already placed Miss Oliver firmly in the mental category of rich bitches. She had met enough of them in her time to recognise the signs early. Spoiled, ill-tempered, utterly indifferent to others.

It didn't promise over-well for the character of Mr Oliver, Senior. He would be either the arrogant male version of his child, or the kind of preoccupied businessman who was too interested in making money to notice what had happened to his sweet little daughter.

She didn't bother wondering about a Mrs Oliver. Carol Clarewell, the owner of her agency, had already informed her that Blaize Oliver had been divorced for something like eight years, and that his ex-wife lived in Monaco.

That, too, was par for the course. Rich people, in Leila's brief experience of them, were all divorced. It was something to do with their money. Money was like plutonium—once a critical mass of the stuff had been amassed, there was inevitably an explosion that blew the first wife to Monaco—or Jersey, or Monte Carlo, as the case might be. The bang usually left one of the partners, in this case evidently the husband, with one or more sulky, maladjusted teenage children.

Hers not to reason why. She was here for six weeks, a top-of-the-range temp who was paid very well to impersonate a computer from nine to five. She wasn't expected to form personal opinions, let alone express them.

Carol Clarewell evidently had a high opinion of the man she'd sent Leila to work for. He owned several companies, and had brought a lot of business Carol's way in the past. She obviously also respected him as a man, however, and that was rare. Carol, a rather overpowering personality, didn't respect many people.

So Leila had been flattered when Carol had passed this job her way. 'It isn't the usual thing,' she'd told Leila. 'He's had some sort of crisis with his personal assistant, and needs a stand-in. He's asked for one of my best people, and that means you.'

They drove through the centre of Barcelona. Even at the speeds Miss Oliver preferred, Leila got the impression of a beautiful city with a unique period atmosphere. During the hour it took to get through the city, Miss Oliver swore at pedestrians twice, changed the cassette for a marginally noisier one, and went through five more sticks of gum. But she didn't address another word to Leila.

Leila, glancing at the girl occasionally, wondered whether she was perhaps even younger than eighteen. Not that it was easy to tell—the nubile Miss Oliver had used a heavy hand with the make-up, and had gone for a sultry, over-sexed look that was very adult. The hands were a giveaway, though. They were girl's hands, dainty and plump, and they bore not the faintest trace of toil.

Leila looked down at her own slender fingers. Plain hands. Hands that had been used to work ever since she could remember. Hands that could type seventy words a minute, and were ringless, short-nailed, and competent. Like the rest of her, they had known a life very different from the cushioned existence of such as young Miss Oliver beside her. Though Leila Thomas was only a few years older than her future employer's daughter, she knew instinctively that she was decades older in experience and maturity.

That's the way it is, she told herself. Now stop dripping acid, and enjoy the ride.

Having passed through the city, the *autopista* climbed steadily upwards, leaving the rather depressing industrial suburbs behind. They passed through a tollgate, and continued on their way up the coast. The countryside around them was suddenly green and flourishing, and the heavy traffic that had dogged them through Barcelona began to ease off.

Though she'd worked in businesses all over England, she'd never been to the Costa Brava before, and she was determined, work and the Olivers permitting, to enjoy her stay here as much as possible.

A red-nailed hand reached out and switched the tape-machine off. In the blissful silence that followed, the girl next to her asked abruptly, 'Is Leila your real name?'

'Yes,' Leila nodded. 'Of course.'

'There's no "of course" about it where secretaries' names are concerned.'

Leila fielded a glance from green eyes that were, she now realised, distinctly hostile. 'Well, my name happens to be Leila.'

'All right. I'd like a talk with you, Miss Leila Thomas.'

'All right.' Leila nodded warily. 'What did you want to say?'

'I wanted to get a few things straight before we get to Cap Sa Sal,' the girl replied, sitting back in the white leather seat to hold the wheel at arm's length.

'Like what?'

'Like keep your hands off my father,' the girl said meaningfully.

'Keep my hands off your——' Leila gaped in surprise. 'What on earth do you mean?'

'Oh, don't treat me like a child!' Miss Oliver snapped. 'Do you think you're the first temporary secretary to come out here? I know what women in your job are like, Miss Thomas.' The colour in her cheeks was deepening as she spoke. 'I'm just warning you—try any tricks with Dad, and I'll see to it that you regret it. Don't think I don't mean it, because I do!'

Leila could only stare at the girl in astonishment. 'Young lady,' she said at last, keeping her voice calm with an effort, 'whatever you think a temp is, you seem to have the wrong end of the stick.'

'Have I?' There was something horribly adult in the cynical expression. 'I don't think so. I had the wrong end of the stick with the last two, but I'm cured now.'

'What do you mean, "the last two"?' Leila asked sharply. 'Are you saying your father had—had some kind of relationship with my predecessors?'

'Oh, you're so sweet and innocent,' the girl sneered. 'Yes, that's exactly what I mean, Miss Thomas. I mean that they trailed their bait, and Dad snapped them up. Only he's not going to snap *you* up. Not this time. There's too much at stake this time!'

Leila was conscious of a sick feeling inside her. Was this precocious teenager telling her the truth about her father? Because, if so, she'd be better off driving herself back to the airport and getting the next plane back to London. She took a deep breath.

'I've come out here to act as personal secretary to your father,' Leila said in a quiet voice. 'I'll be here for six weeks. I do audio typing, shorthand and word processing. Nothing else. *Nothing* else,' she repeated meaningfully. 'After this job, I go home, and get my next assignment with the next firm. I never get involved with my employers on a personal level, and I've never yet come across one who wanted to get involved with me.'

'Well, just make sure you mean that.'

'Listen, Miss Oliver, I'm not a great deal older than you—— '

'Don't kid yourself!' Miss Oliver retorted contemptuously. 'You're at least twenty-three or twenty-four, right? I'm fifteen.'

'Fifteen?' Her guess had been out by three years! And the girl was right—she was nine years older. It occurred to Leila to wonder angrily what kind of father would let his fifteen-year-old daughter dress like this, talk like this to strangers, not to mention——

'Have you got a licence to drive this car?' Leila asked briskly as the thought occurred to her.

She got a sly glance back. 'Don't be stupid.'

'I'm not being stupid, Miss Oliver,' Leila replied, tight-lipped. 'If you think I'm impressed, I assure you I'm not. I think the best thing will be if you pull into the next service station that comes up, and let me drive the rest of the way.'

'Like hell,' the teenager said, turning to stare at Leila incredulously. 'Nobody drives this car but me!'

'You shouldn't even be driving a scooter. I'd like you to drop me off, please,' Leila said evenly.

Something in the steely note of her voice had got through to the girl. Unconsciously, her foot had eased on the accelerator, slowing their hectic pace. 'Does my driving scare you that much?' she asked defiantly.

'Frankly, yes,' Leila replied. 'But your not having a licence is far more serious. You see, I *do* have a licence,

and I want to keep it. And if the traffic police stop us
for any reason, they'll hold me directly responsible for
your recklessness. I don't know how you've got this car,
or what your father lets you do with it, but I'm not prepared to risk my licence. It's vital to my work, and my
work is my livelihood. So, if you'll let me out at this
service station coming up, I'm sure I'll be able to organise
my own transport to your father's house.'

'Now, come on——'

'I mean it,' Leila said grimly. 'Pull in.'

For a moment, she thought that the girl wasn't going
to obey, and she wondered anxiously just what the hell
she would do if her bluff were called. But, at the last
minute, Miss Oliver swung the Golf off the motorway
and on to the slip-road that led to the service station car
park. Her jaw was clenched, and her cheeks wore ugly
blotches of colour. She pulled up so sharply that Leila
had to put a hand out to stop herself sliding into the
dashboard.

She turned to face Leila, her eyes narrowed. 'All right.
You drive from here on.'

Leila silenced her own sigh of relief. 'Thank you.' She
got out of the car, and walked round to the driver's side.

As they exchanged places, Leila stared sharply at the
girl, and wondered how she could ever have been fooled.
This girl was an adolescent; though she was physically
almost mature, with her full figure and burgeoning sexual
allure, the look in her eyes was not that of a grown-up.
Especially not now that they were hot and sullen with
defeat.

It was the hair, Leila decided, that had most fooled
her. Worn in the sculpted masses of a soap-opera star,
it had given an air of instant maturity to a face that was,
as yet, still too rounded and unformed to be that of an
adult woman.

She tried to hide the way her nose had started to
wrinkle in disgust at the kind of household that would

permit a teenager to get herself up like this, and drive sixty miles on the motorway to pick up an employee. What kind of family was she coming to stay among? There was a bad taste in her mouth as she held up her palm.

'The keys, please.'

'I'll be watching you,' the girl said meaningfully. 'I may be too young to drive, but I'm not too young to know about people.' She tossed the keys on to Leila's lap. Leila fitted them into the ignition, but didn't start the car.

'You said there was too much at stake,' she said heavily, watching the girl's sullen face. 'Would you mind telling me what all this is about?'

'It's about me and Terry standing up for ourselves for once in our lives,' the girl shot back. 'Since the divorce, we haven't had a mother. We haven't had a family at all, since I was a kid!'

'I'm sorry to hear that,' Leila replied quietly.

'Oh, Dad's very good at picking up women,' the girl said with a painful sneer, 'but not the kind who stick around. Know what I mean? Until Katherine.'

'Who is Katherine?' Leila asked.

'She's the woman my father's going to marry,' came the confident reply. 'And if you get in the way, Miss Thomas, or do anything to come between them, I'll——' she clenched her plump hands, her breathing unsteady '—I'll kill myself!'

In the silence, the roar of traffic on the *autopista* was a distant drone through the closed windows. Just what the hell was she doing here, staring at this emotional, mixed-up kid, who was so sure Leila had designs on her father?

'I take it,' she said slowly, 'that Terry is your brother.'

'He's nine.' Suddenly, the green eyes were swimming with tears between the fringe of mascara-coated lashes.

'He's n-nine, and he's never had any other m-mother than me. He deserves something better...'

Leila didn't offer her hanky or make any other gesture of comfort as the sentence dissolved. Oddly, Miss Oliver was far more womanly in her tears than she ever had been in her brazenness. It was starting to dawn on Leila that all this—the make-up, the aggression, perhaps even taking the car—had been designed especially for her benefit this morning.

She looked out of the window, listening to the choked sounds of Miss Oliver wrestling for self-control beside her.

So Mr Blaize Oliver had enjoyed affairs with the last two temps who'd come out to work for him. Who had only been three out of a long line of women he'd seduced and discarded. And, all the time, his two children had been tormented, to the extent that his fifteen-year-old daughter had been driven to pitting her own immature wits against the latest intruder...

Mr Oliver sounded a beaut.

Leila turned to look at the girl at last, who was sniffing miserably. Her mascara had smudged tragically down one cheek, and she looked less than twelve. All traces of adulthood were melting fast.

'What's your first name?' Leila asked gently.

'Tr-Tracey.'

'OK, Tracey. There's a wash-room over there. I want you to go and rinse all that stuff off your face. When you're ready, come and join me in the restaurant, and we'll have a cup of coffee. Yes?'

'Yes.' Tracey nodded. With a shaky sigh that went straight to Leila's heart, she reached over and took an overnight bag off the back seat. 'My proper clothes,' she said dully, in answer to Leila's glance. 'Dad would kill me if he saw me wearing this outfit.'

'Ah.'

She watched the girl walk to the wash-room. She had poise, at any rate. She walked in the high heels with not a hint of clumsiness, and her tumbled head was held high.

Shaking away the pity, Leila made her own way to the restaurant. The very last thing she needed right now was to get involved in some awful intra-family row. When this girl got back, she would impress upon her that she had *no* designs on her father, and that she was just here to do her job.

And then she would leave it at that.

There was no room in this job, or in Leila Thomas's life, for the luxury of compassion. Or even, she reminded herself sharply, the luxury of feeling anger against an employer. Whatever kind of a bastard Blaize Oliver was, he meant nothing to her. If he made a pass at her, which he surely would, she knew how to deflect it.

She'd learned all about that long ago. It sometimes took men a little time to appreciate Leila's quiet, understated beauty, but it was there, none the less. And when you'd grown up alone, poor, and largely defence-less, you soon realised what pigs some men could be.

Maybe that was why she'd been able to cut through Tracey Oliver's act, where another woman might have been daunted. At Tracey's age she'd also had to defend herself, and pretend she was far more adult than she was. And she had also ached for a mother with that hollow, constant pain.

She knew what that felt like, all right. Although those days were a long way back in her past, and her present was now coloured by a touch of luxury—even of glamour—she would never forget the lessons she'd learned then.

So, if Blaize Oliver, international businessman and rake, were to try any of his well-practised charm on her, she knew exactly how to react.

She sat down, waiting for the girl. Her appearance in the busy restaurant, all alone, had already attracted male eyes. Perhaps that was just because her clothes were subtly wrong for this climate. The cotton blouse had seemed cool in London. Here, especially after the last five minutes with Tracey, it was sticking to her back. And the skirt was too heavy. Tracey had been right; the Costa Brava in July was not a place for anything but the lightest of wear.

Thank goodness she'd had her hair cut short before leaving London. Assuming she'd be washing it frequently for the next six weeks, she'd sacrificed a mass of silvery gold that most women would have considered a priceless treasure. But the short page-boy cut was a lot more practical than, if not as pretty as, the platinum tresses she'd left behind. It also kept her profile lower, which was something she'd learned to cultivate as a top-flight secretary. For the same reason, her full, leaf-shaped mouth wore a shade of lipstick that was deliberately dull, just as the tan eye-shadow helped tone down the vivid blue of her eyes. Discretion was something to be prized; she wasn't in the business of pleasing male eyes.

At first, she hardly recognised the girl who had come to stand at her table, clutching an overnight bag. Then her blue eyes widened.

As a tarted-up nymphet, Tracey Oliver had been pretty. Scrubbed down to a fifteen-year-old child, she was ravishing. She'd brushed the chestnut mane of hair out of its sculpted waves, and it now cloudily framed the wistful face of a Renaissance angel in a Siennese masterpiece. She was wearing faded jeans and a yellow tank top, with pink trainers. Universal teenager-wear. It showed her pretty figure off, but not in the way the leather skirt and high heels had done.

Only the eyes were the same—deep green and deeply confused.

'Sit down,' Leila invited. 'I'll get us two coffees. Want a piece of cake or a sandwich?'

'You won't have any Spanish money.' Tracey said practically. 'I'll get them. Want an *ensaimada*?'

'I'll risk it,' Leila said with a faint smile. The girl dumped her bag, and went off to the counter. Leila watched her, marvelling at the change. What kind of man could let an exquisite child like this suffer and go to seed? Was Blaize Oliver so selfish, or so indifferent, that he couldn't see what his life-style was doing to his children?

One of these days the wind would change, and then the garish tart in the red leather skirt would really be Tracey Oliver. And not all of her father's money would be able to scrub the paint away again.

Tracey had played the part superbly. From how many cheap women had she learned that style, that cutting and dismissive manner?

Leila felt bitter anger uncoil inside her, but only for a moment. She was a professional secretary, not a social worker. She was here to get through the next month and a half, not to make moral judgements on the lives of others.

Tracey had returned with a tray. The *ensaimada* turned out to be a curly bun with a filling of delicious confectioner's cream. Tracey had bought herself one, too, and she ate with a teenager's purposeful hunger, gulping her coffee down. The marks of her recent tears were still there, but fading, to leave only faint bruises under those vivid green eyes.

'Tracey is a very pretty name,' Leila began when the girl had finished. 'When I was your age, it was one of the names I wanted to be called.'

'Really?' Tracey meditated. 'But Leila is a lovely name.'

'I didn't like it, not then. Anyway, it's a Persian name, meaning dark, so it couldn't have been more inaccurate.'

Tracey cupped her chin in her hands, and considered Leila's hair. 'It's real?'

'As real as the rest of me. And I was even blonder then. Anyway, maybe I'll grow into my name one of these days. Does your father really let you drive the car on the motorway?'

'He'd kill me if he found out.' It was the second time she'd used that phrase, and it didn't escape Leila. 'He thinks the chauffeur dropped me off at the beach this morning. But I gave him twenty thousand pesetas to let me take the car to the airport, instead.'

'That sounds an awful lot of pesetas.'

'No, it's only a hundred quid.' Tracey shrugged the sum off with a rich girl's indifference to money. 'He's not a regular chauffeur. He's really just the gardener, and he needs the money.'

'I see.' Rich kids were very good at spotting that quality in underlings. Leila leaned forward. 'Listen, Tracey. I think I understand why you did what you did this morning. But you didn't need to do any of it. I've got no intentions of getting involved with your father. Absolutely none, I swear it. I've never even met him, and, whatever those other agency women were like, most temps are just like me—hard-working and only interested in doing their job. I want you to believe that.'

The girl was picking at a loose thread on her jeans as she listened. 'You haven't met Dad,' she said without looking up.

'I'm sure your dad is an attractive man,' Leila said gently. 'But I'm not looking for a man, especially not——' She was about to say *the kind of man your father is*, but the girl had looked up quickly, and she amended her sentence. 'Especially not at this stage of my life. I just want to get ahead in my job. Believe me, I really hope your father and this lady you like, Katherine, get together.' She hesitated. 'Don't be too disappointed if it doesn't work out. People have to run their own lives——'

'It *will* work out,' the girl said fiercely, with a touch of her old autocratic manner.

'OK,' Leila nodded, noting the intent in the blazing green eyes. 'It will work out. Just believe me when I say that I'm not here to come between your father and Katherine. I'm an employee, a very temporary one. And I'd like us to be friends for the next six weeks, if that's possible. If not, then I hope at least we won't be enemies.'

She'd said enough. She finished her coffee, and checked her watch. She'd never driven on the Continent before, let alone in a left-hand-drive car, and they couldn't be more than a third of the way to Cap Sa Sal. There was a lot of motorway ahead of them.

Today hadn't exactly been a shiningly auspicious beginning to this assignment. She was hoping devoutly that things would start going a bit better from now on.

When she looked up, Tracey was watching her with those cloudy green eyes.

'Shall we go?' Leila invited mildly.

Tracey's knuckles were pale around the handle of the bag. 'I guess you think I'm a terrible brat.'

'No,' Leila said calmly, rising. 'You're just a woman defending her family. I understand that perfectly.'

For a moment, the girl looked surprised. Then her mouth flickered momentarily into a rather bruised and tentative smile. It was not a smile that said she believed any of Leila's promises, or even that she felt friendly towards her. It was the instinctive smile of a child who had been understood, and who wasn't understood very often.

'OK,' she said. 'Let's go. I'll show you the way.'

The drive up to the house was impressive—not just because it was over half a mile of tarmac, bordered with needle cypresses, but because, in its winding convolutions, it gave some spectacular views of the sea to one side, and the hilltop castle of a small town on the other.

The house itself came into view during the last few hundred yards. It was an enchantingly beautiful property, an old Catalan farmhouse whose ancient stones had been cloaked in ivy. The garden around it was a fabulous tangle of flowering shrubs and trees, bordering an expanse of emerald lawn, over which sprinklers played a rain of diamonds.

She'd expected money, but not taste. In fact, this place was a world away from the new white villa with ostentatious tennis-court and swimming-pool which she'd been expecting. This was a place of singular beauty, a place that made you ache for its loveliness.

'Let me out here,' Tracey commanded as they breasted the rise. 'Go round the back of the house, and park under the trellis thing. Then go round to the front door. I'll meet you there.' Pleading green eyes turned to her. 'Don't let Dad know I drove to meet you, please.'

'I won't.'

'Don't tell the governess, either. She's a snitch.'

'OK.' Leila let the teenager out, watched her disappear into the garden, then drove on as she'd been directed. What a place! The views from up here, just to round everything off, were incomparable—a vista of curving bays that stretched towards the flawless horizon.

The 'trellis thing' turned out to be a huge pergola over which a wistaria was in breathtaking purple blossom, trailing its heavy flower-heads almost to the roofs of the cars. She parked next to a black Porsche 911 and a well-used Jeep, and got out, stretching herself. The drive had been tense, but this was worth a dozen such drives.

Carrying only her shoulder-bag, she walked round the house, as Tracey had commanded. The impression of weathered age was deceptive; her quick eye noticed well-made new windows, new guttering, and smart new lights set into the venerable walls. Somewhere not far off, a big dog was barking, but she made it to the front door unmolested, and rang the bell.

Tracey Oliver was only slightly out of breath as she opened the door.

'Dad's in the pool,' she announced. 'I'll take you through to see him. Pedro's getting your bags out of the car.'

'Pedro's the needy chauffeur, I suppose?'

Tracey nodded. 'He's more greedy than needy. Greedy people give me the creeps. Don't bump into any of this junk, it's worth a fortune.'

The junk in question was a large collection of oil-paintings, marble busts, statuettes and Chinese porcelain which stood haphazardly in the hallway, like the preparations for a very, very expensive jumble sale. 'Stuff from England,' Tracey explained dismissively. 'Dad went on a shopping spree to furnish this place.'

'Some shopping spree!'

'Sotheby's and Christie's.' She pulled a face. 'I hate all this old musty stuff. I wanted to do the house all white inside. White floors, white walls, white furniture. But no one ever listens to me.'

As she followed Tracey through the house, Leila decided that Blaize Oliver had, at least, better taste than his daughter. The house was obviously still in the process of being furnished, but what had been put in so far was very beautiful, and revealed a rich, wide-ranging taste— the kind of taste that needed a very long purse to finance it. By the looks of it, Mr Oliver hadn't put a foot wrong so far. The place was going to be stunning, from the Murano crystal chandeliers hanging from the ceilings to the Aubusson carpets on the tiled floors.

'You haven't been here very long, then?' Leila questioned.

'Dad bought the place a month ago,' Tracey volunteered. 'It's just a holiday place, of course, but Dad tends to go over the top.'

Just a *holiday* place? That really made Leila rock for a moment. What in heaven's name was this family's permanent dwelling like?

Tracey led the way through a vast, superbly equipped kitchen out into a side garden, where yet another emerald sweep of lawn glittered under a rain of automatic sprinklers.

The pool was a sheet of turquoise beyond the lawn, bordered by unreal rows of white columns, supporting another pergola, this time of scarlet trumpet vine. They skirted the sprinklers, and walked to the edge of the pool. A white towelling robe was slung over one of a pair of white garden chairs. On the table next to it were half a dozen newspapers, two telephones plugged into an extension socket, and a large jug of orange juice with two glasses.

A darkly tanned man was swimming lazily up and down in the blue water, with the easy power of a battle-cruiser. Tracey slid into the vacant chair, and glanced at Leila with assessing green eyes.

'He'll see us in a minute. Want some orange juice? It's freshly squeezed.'

'No, thanks.'

Feeling oddly tense, Leila waited at the edge of the water, holding her shoulder-bag in both hands. Sure enough, the swimmer turned at the far end, and made an arrow-straight track towards where she stood. Reaching the edge of the pool, he hauled himself out with a ripple of wet bronze muscle, and flicked the water from his long dark hair.

A fist clenched around Leila's heart.

She was looking into the face of the most devastatingly handsome man she had ever seen in her life.

CHAPTER TWO

LEILA had seen those green eyes before, in the face of his daughter. But where Tracey Oliver's eyes were gentle and wistful, Blaize Oliver's eyes were as hard and brilliant as that rarest of stones, a green diamond. They reminded Leila of the eyes of a tiger she had once seen in a zoo.

Their stare was awesome, made shockingly sexual by the thick black lashes that fringed them. A straight Roman nose and powerful cheekbones surmounted a mouth that was soul-dissolvingly passionate, with a full lower lip, holding both cruelty and sensuality. It was impossible for Leila to look at that mouth and not wonder what it would feel like pressed against her own. Blaize Oliver had the kind of beauty that exploded the most prepared poise, and violated the vulnerable feminine sensibilities beneath.

'Mr Oliver?' she said unsteadily. 'I'm Leila Thomas, from the Clarewell Agency.'

'I know.' The green stare weighed her up. 'You come highly recommended, Miss Thomas.'

'If so, I'll do my best to earn it,' she answered without smiling.

'I hope so,' he said, his voice deep and husky, with a distinctive, dryish note. 'I make demands on my staff, and I expect them to come up to scratch. Always.'

She thought of what Tracey had told her. 'I've come here to work, Mr Oliver,' she said significantly.

His smile was mocking. 'Was there any doubt about that?'

23

'Not as far as *I'm* concerned,' she said, with a slight emphasis, and wondered whether he'd got the message now.

Blaize Oliver was in his late thirties, maybe as old as forty; yet she'd never seen a younger man who could compare with him. In fact, every man she'd ever met had been just a pale imitation of this one.

The hair that was slicked back wetly from his high temples was very dark, but not quite black, and free of any touch of silver. And the rest of him was equally, magnificently male. His skin was fine, and tanned the rich colour of newly poured bronze. Crisp, dark hair etched the broad chest and lean rib-cage, delineating the supple muscles of his stomach, and streaking the long, lean thighs.

It was suddenly a lot easier to understand the helpless desperation of Tracey Oliver. This was a man who could have any woman he chose, just by snapping his fingers.

She tore her eyes away from the physically stunning man in front of her, and found herself looking into the cynical eyes of Tracey Oliver, who was watching her with weary irony from the chair. 'You haven't met Dad.' The sentence rose unbidden out of her unconscious.

Gulping down the tense lump in her throat, she said, 'I'm ready to start any time. Where would you like me to begin?'

'This afternoon will do.' He picked up a towel, and dried his face and hair briskly. Leila waited in silence, watching the way muscles flickered under his tanned skin. Tracey was still sitting in silence, her eyes moving from Leila to her father alternately. 'Know anything about me?' he asked as he dried himself.

Leila cleared her throat. 'You run a multinational,' she replied.

'I *own* a multinational.' He made the distinction calmly. 'I pay a great many other people to run it. I don't suppose you know why you're here, either?'

'No,' she said.

'I sacked my personal assistant some weeks ago,' he told her coolly. 'My staff, who seem to feel this is some kind of disaster, are frantically finding a replacement. Up till now, no one's turned up with the right qualifications. You're here to stop the gap until the right person *does* turn up. Carol Clarewell tells me that you've picked up a good grasp of how big businesses run, along the line.'

'I'm not a genius, by any means. But I've worked in big firms before.'

'Well, given the glowing reference Carol has furnished me with, I doubt whether the work here will prove either very onerous for you, or will adequately fill your time. I don't expect you to undertake any company work, just routine secretarial stuff. There's a certain amount of work that's inevitable. But I expect you to make sure that no unnecessary hassle ends up on my plate. I'm on vacation right now. With my family. I intend the next six weeks to be as close to a holiday as my cluttered life is able to achieve, for my children and for me.'

'That's understood,' Leila nodded, thinking cynically that his family-man image didn't fit very well with the silent child who was watching them.

'Good.' He reached out then, took her arm in cool, strong fingers, and lifted it slightly. 'You're as pale as ivory,' he said. 'You need some Spanish sun, urgently.'

He was inspecting her with no less interest than she had been inspecting him, his eyes undressing her with unashamed interest, assessing the curves of her woman's body, and obviously appraising her potential to interest him in bed. A sudden rush of heat, which had nothing to do with the sun, prickled across her skin.

'I hope you've brought a bathing costume?'

'Well—yes, I've brought one——'

'You're going to need it. I do a lot of work out here by the pool.'

Leila glanced swiftly at Tracey, but Tracey was looking steadfastly away, her full mouth tight and compressed. The ugly blotches were back in her smooth cheeks. Leila winced inwardly for the girl.

Blaize Oliver sat down on the reclining chair, and slipped dark glasses over his eyes. He lay back nonchalantly, trailing his fingers down his own flat belly, chasing water droplets idly. She tried not to look at him, at the supple contours of his torso.

'Has Tracey shown you your room yet?' he asked.

'No.'

'She'll show you now. Won't you, Trace?'

'Yes, Dad.'

'If you have any complaints, Miss Thomas, let me know.'

'I'm sure I won't have any complaints.'

He tilted his head at her, and slid his dark glasses down just far enough to be able to smile into her eyes. 'No. You're not the complaining type, are you, Miss Thomas?' He slid the sun-glasses back over his eyes. 'Lunch is in an hour. You must be eager to freshen up before then.'

'I'd like a shower.' Leila nodded.

'After that motorway, you'll need one. Tracey, show Miss Thomas to her room, and then you'd better finish off those sums we were doing last night.'

'Oh, Dad——'

'Oh, Dad, nothing. Get them done before you forget everything I showed you.'

'Can't I have a swim before lunch?'

'After spending all morning on the beach?'

'Please, Dad!'

'Sums,' he repeated firmly. 'Show our guest to her room, and then spend half an hour in your study. And don't disturb Terry.'

'Where is he?'

'In his room. He threw a tantrum for Lucy's benefit, and I won't abide tantrums.'

'Can't I do my sums tonight?'

'Tracey!' The change in Blaize Oliver's voice was slight, but it was enough to silence the girl at once. 'Yes, Dad.' She uncoiled her body from the chair, and gave Leila a look that was cold and empty.

'Follow me, Miss Thomas.'

The room she had been given was a very pretty little suite, with its own white and gold bathroom, and a window opening out over a mass of flowers in the garden. The walls were crowded with paintings, and the terra-cotta-tiled floor was so invitingly cool in this heat that Leila kicked her shoes off and padded around barefoot as she explored.

She had her own television, her own music centre, complete with records—mainly classical, which suited her fine—and even her own little library, complete with thrillers, romances and a row of recent autobiographies.

Deciding that she was going to be more than comfortable here, she put Mozart on the turntable, and undressed for her shower.

What a stunning man Blaize Oliver was! Yet so arrogant, so used to the world revolving around him. She remembered those lazy fingers tracing water on his own bare skin. He'd made an impact on Leila that was still reverberating inside her.

When she'd faced him at the pool this morning, she'd been aware of a feeling she'd never had before. A sudden wish that, instead of being a humble employee turning up for a month and a half of drudgery here, she was a guest. A woman of style and background, arriving on the same level as Blaize Oliver. Someone he would learn to know, someone he would treat like an equal...

But, of course, he must make a lot of women feel like that. She'd known handsome men who hadn't possessed an ounce of charisma, and she'd known plain men who had more than their share of sexual magnetism. But this combination of the two was nothing short of overwhelming. No wonder his children were getting desperate at the procession of impermanent women who passed through their lives. Poor Tracey. Poor Terry. Poor little kids.

Forget them. Forget Blaize Oliver. Just be here, now.

She soaped her skin, deliberately keeping the water just off cold, enjoying the sensation of heat and grime rinsing away.

If she was a sensualist, then her senses craved only this kind of gratification: to be cool and clean, to stand under a shower, or to lie on crisp white sand. To put on fresh linen and to sleep between clean sheets. To feel the wind through her hair, to breathe in the scent of pine trees.

Leila's body was slender, the body of a woman who avoided excess. There was no spare fat in any of the treacherous places that could make even so slight a woman as Leila seem heavy. The long, balletic muscles of her legs and waist counterbalanced the naturally feminine arches of her hips and bust; and, although the curves of her breasts were full, they were light and taut, tipped with the pale pink nipples that went with very fair skin.

She dried herself, glowingly naked in the richly furnished room, and gave her reflection in the cheval-glass a quick check-over. What had Blaize Oliver seen that had struck him as so delicious? The lightness of her colouring was almost a gleam. Her bright cap of hair framed a face that was wide across the cheekbones, curving to a small, decisive chin. The space between was occupied by wide, deep blue eyes, a wide, deep pink mouth, and a short, straight nose.

The combination could have been sweetly innocuous. But the determination that sat on the mouth, and the experience that deepened the eyes, made it a unique face, with its own unique beauty.

Men usually looked twice, as if to confirm that their first impression had not been mistaken. They very seldom got an alluring look in return. Leila was not, and had never been, a woman who courted men's glances. Compliments like the ones Mr Oliver's eyes and mouth had given her this morning tended not to register.

She'd worked grindingly hard to get where she was now. To consistently find work in an agency like Carol Clarewell's you had to have more than just finely sharpened secretarial skills. You had to have ambition, drive, determination. You had to have the durability that put you one step ahead of the rest.

And, in exchange, you got three things: the highest salaries in the business, which meant a lot to a girl who'd once been desolately poor, the chance to travel, which filled some longing deep in her heart, and a career without permanent commitments, which was a bonus to someone who'd been disillusioned and betrayed as often as Leila Thomas had.

To be able to walk out of any assignment, if she were ill-treated. Not to have to submit to any bullying, sexual or otherwise, in order to keep a job. To change bosses and environments long before they palled on her—these were priceless aspects of her job to Leila. She didn't want commitments. Since Carol had taken her on three years ago, she hadn't stayed with one employer for more than three months at a time, and that was exactly the way she liked it.

She spanned her taut waist with her hands, her fingertips almost meeting on either side of her smooth navel. Twenty-four was a good age to be. She was happy with her life, and that was something that hadn't been true for twenty-one out of those twenty-four years.

She put on a lightweight sun-dress in a bright synthetic print, slipped sandals on her bare feet, and went down the wide staircase for lunch.

There seemed to be a lot of people at lunch, which was served at a long oak table in the high-ceilinged, cool dining-room. Leila had been placed at the end of the table, opposite Blaize Oliver, who was now wearing a patterned shirt and faded jeans. The amused green eyes met hers once or twice during the meal, as though he was enjoying a joke she hadn't caught yet.

Terry Oliver sat beside his sister. The boy barely raised his eyes from his plate, picking at his food with an indifference that made Leila look pityingly at his skinny arms and lean, sulky face. Whatever sin he had committed to have earned imprisonment all morning, he didn't have the air of a penitent now. He announced glumly that he had a cold, which he confirmed by sneezing several times during the meal and blowing his nose awkwardly on a spotless white hanky. Tracey, too, spoke little during the meal, though her appetite was ravenous.

Two Englishwomen sitting next to the children turned out to be a governess and a housekeeper. Miss Lucy, the governess, was young, and talked animatedly to Leila in a bright South London accent. Mrs Saunders, the housekeeper, was elderly, and did not. She looked grimly efficient, at least. Leila wondered how well the voluble Miss Lucy could be doing her job if she couldn't control Terry's tantrums, and if Tracey had given her the slip so easily that morning. She assumed drily that a pretty face and a sexy figure had gone a long way towards getting her the job.

There were two other men at the table. One, a middle-aged Spaniard, appeared to be a friend, and talked energetically in Spanish to Blaize. The other was a good-looking American in his mid-twenties, who sat beside Leila, and introduced himself as Rick Watermeyer.

Leila's curiosity was disappointed, however, to register that there was no sign of Katherine, the woman whom Tracey was so keen to enlist as stepmother.

'Are you with Mr Oliver's company?' she asked Rick Watermeyer politely.

'Not exactly.' He smiled. 'I'm Blaize's pilot and flying instructor.'

'Is Mr Oliver learning to fly his own plane?' she asked.

'Helicopter,' Rick corrected mildly. 'Blaize learned to fly fixed-wing two years ago. I'm teaching him to fly a neat little Gadfly he bought this year. Once he's got his licence I'll go back to the flying school where I usually work, just outside Manchester. In the meantime, I'm having a whale of a time here.'

'It's certainly very beautiful,' Leila said. 'I imagine a helicopter is the perfect way to get around this rocky coastline.'

'Oh, sure.' Rick smiled. 'And they're great for getting around cities, too. Choppers have a lot of advantages for a man like Blaize.' He leaned forward confidentially. 'A guy in his position can't afford to take hours getting where he wants to go, you know.'

'I'm sure he can't,' Leila said drily. 'Mr Oliver has to get what he wants as soon as possible, doesn't he?'

'Right. There's no problem with landing-strips, either,' Rick said, missing her irony. 'You can put a chopper down wherever there's a bit of lawn or a stretch of tarmac. They're fast, and they get you exactly where you want to go. We can even put the Gadfly down on top of the office-building, in London.'

'It's fabulous,' Lucy sighed, passing Leila a dish of prawns. 'I love being in helicopters. When they take off, it *does* something to your insides.' Her eyes were bright. 'I can't get enough of it, and yet I hate ordinary flying. Isn't that funny?'

'I imagine the children love it, too,' Leila said conversationally. Terry looked up quickly from his plate, his green eyes, so like his sister's and father's, showing a flicker of bitterness. He sneezed into his hanky.

'Oh, no,' Lucy said, dabbing her mouth. 'The children have never been up. Mr Oliver wouldn't permit it.'

'Why not?'

'It costs a fortune to keep the helicopter up, doesn't it, Rick?'

'It isn't cheap,' Rick agreed.

'And Mr Oliver says that a helicopter isn't a toy,' Lucy smiled. 'Drink your milk up, Terry. You know it's good for you, especially when you've got a bit of a cold.'

'I see,' Leila said quietly. The toys were all for adults in this household, it seemed. The selfishness of the man was evident in everything he did. She was no stranger to the world of the rich. Most of the people she'd temped for were concerned with making a lot of money as fast as possible. But Blaize Oliver was different. Not yet forty, he had already made more money—or more likely inherited it—than he knew how to spend, and was simply living among his wealth with casual enjoyment. He could buy helicopters, and keep an instructor on tap, with the nonchalance with which ordinary people bought a house-plant.

And, in the midst of all this opulence, his two children sat as quiet and ignored as mice. It hadn't escaped her notice that Blaize hadn't spoken to his children, or paid them any sort of attention, through the whole course of the meal.

Lunch broke up shortly before two, with everyone moving off to different duties or enjoyments. Leila waited at the table for orders from her employer, picking idly at a bunch of grapes.

Turning from the Spaniard with a laugh, he came over to Leila. 'Ready for a little work?'

'Of course.' She nodded.

He towered over her, looking down at her. 'Go and get your costume on, then. I'll see you out at the pool.' It was none the less a command for being said easily.

She touched the cool sun-dress she'd changed into after her shower. 'Actually, I'm fine in what I've got on——'

'You'll roast,' he cut through her protests calmly. 'This is the hottest part of the day. Besides, you'll get splashed.' His eyes glittered that hidden smile. 'I'm a boisterous swimmer, Miss Thomas.'

'Well, I don't mind the odd splash——'

'And bring a notepad. We'll kick off with some letters, and then see what the afternoon's phone calls bring in. Later tonight, I'll show you the office where you can use the computers and the telex.'

'Very well.'

'Move it, then.'

'Mr Oliver,' she said with an effort, 'I'd really rather stay in my dress, if it's all the same to you.'

'But it isn't all the same to me. Lesson number one.' The force of his personality was underlined by the gentle, husky tone. 'Complete obedience. At all times. Go and change, Miss Thomas.'

He walked away, leaving her fuming in her chair. Abruptly, she noticed Tracey's tense face watching her from across the table.

'Come along, Miss Thomas.' Tracey's voice was thin, and her eyes had that bruised look again. 'What are you waiting for? Get yourself into your costume, like a good little temp. Dad's keen to examine the wares, can't you see that?'

Leila suppressed her flash of anger, and went upstairs without a word.

The costume she'd bought before leaving London had not been designed for lying in the sun in the full view of her employer.

She'd always strictly divided her clothes into on-duty and off-duty, and the dusky pink bikini was very definitely an off-duty garment. It belonged to the other side of her life, the side that didn't have to bother being discreet, or keeping a low profile. She'd bought it to get the maximum amount of tan in her off-duty hours. Alone.

It was bad enough that the halter-neck top clung to her neat, full breasts rather too lovingly. It was worse that the bottom was cut so high at the hip that it was no more than two triangles of pink nylon. The bikini didn't so much cover her femininity as flaunt it with a fanfare of trumpets. Leila realised with despair as she checked her reflection in the mirror that a man like Blaize Oliver would take it as a blatant invitation. 'Dad's keen to examine the wares.' And Tracey would feel exactly the same way. After all her promises to the girl this morning, it was going to look as though she were deliberately setting out to attract attention.

She looked away from her reflection, across the room. Through the window, the riotous garden blossomed, nature flourishing in all its exuberance. And, beyond, that violet-blue sky.

What the hell! She hadn't come here to get involved with anyone. Her life was her own, and no one else's. She had no reason to feel guilt about anything. She was a professional, wasn't she? Why should she let herself get embroiled in the spider's web of emotions that was stretched around this house? If her employer wanted her to work in a bikini, or in yellow overalls, what was that to her?

Angrily, Leila belted the matching towelling robe around her waist, picked up a steno pad and pencil, and walked out of the room to meet her employer.

Blaize Oliver was waiting for her at the edge of the pool, reclining in one of the white chairs, talking brusquely down the telephone. A cup of coffee was going cold on the table in front of him. He was back in his swimming-trunks, but had a white robe slung carelessly around his shoulders. A muscular arm reached out and hauled the other chair close to his own. He covered the mouthpiece for a moment.

'Take that robe off and sit down,' he commanded her, then went back on a rapid-fire of quick instructions down the telephone.

Leila obeyed, willing her poise not to falter as she did so. The sun was suddenly hot on her skin. She was all too aware of the man's eyes on her as she sat, and poised the pencil over the pad.

'And tell Milan I want the whole thing wrapped up by September,' he concluded. 'Impress on them that, strikes or no strikes, if they can't deliver I'll find someone who can. Call me back, Steve.'

He dropped the receiver, and gave his full attention to Leila. 'Well, well.' His voice was cool. 'So that's what you've been hiding under those drab clothes?' He was studying her creamy body with lazy interest. 'You're well put together, Miss Thomas.'

Leila flushed. 'I'm ready to start work, Mr Oliver.'

'So am I.' He nodded, eyes hooded. 'If you want to take that top off, please don't be shy. Everyone sun-bathes topless round here.'

Her flush deepened. 'That really won't be necessary, thank you. Where do you want to begin?'

She knew he was laughing at her, and she hated him for it. The sensual mouth curved in a mocking smile. 'How fast can you take dictation?'

'Fast,' she said succinctly, pencil poised over the pad.

'Very well. Tell me if you want me to slow down.'

And he launched into the afternoon's work.

'But, darling,' Katherine Henessey said in her smooth, sweet voice, 'it's not as if they're real stones. And all young girls are wearing pretty things these days. It's the fashion.'

'That bracelet was expensive,' Blaize said firmly. 'You shouldn't have bought it for her. I don't want my kids spoiled, you know that.'

'Oh, you're too strict,' Katherine protested.

'Tracey gets everything she asks for,' Blaize replied drily. 'That isn't good for a girl of her age.'

'I was spoiled rotten as a girl, and *I've* turned out all right. Besides, Tracey's as quiet as a mouse. She needs a little spoiling.' Katherine turned to Leila for support. 'Am I right, Leila?'

They were sitting in a relaxed group on the terrace, after a late dinner. A few candles glowed on the tables, but most of the illumination was coming from the millions of diamond-bright stars that spangled the velvet sky above. It was balmy and warm. Over the two days she'd been here, Leila hadn't felt cold once; in fact, right now her shoulders were prickling with the painful itch of incipient sunburn. Too late, she'd realised that a wide-brimmed hat was essential wear in this Spanish sun.

She just smiled in answer to Katherine's question. It wasn't hard to see why Tracey Oliver was so keen on this tall, willowy neighbour from across the valley. Katherine Henessey, a tall, brunette divorcee in her mid-thirties, paid both children the kind of attention that they so obviously craved. She'd been here most of the evening, and the children had blossomed in her company tonight. It had been almost pathetic to see their faces lit up with laughter for once, and to see Tracey's pleasure in the pretty little bracelet that Katherine had brought for her. When they'd been packed off to bed, both children had kissed Katherine goodnight with real affection.

Whether that affection was truly reciprocated or not, Leila felt uncertain. There were certain resonances to

Katherine Henessey that she found somehow contrived, too sweet for belief.

Or was she just showing the cynicism of someone who'd never known unalloyed kindness from a stranger? Perhaps she was. But, whatever Tracey's views on the matter, Leila knew with a woman's instinct that Katherine Henessey was very serious about Blaize. It was obvious, because she made it so *un*obvious.

Katherine was on terms of easy familiarity with the family, whom she'd known in England for a year or two; it had been Katherine, Leila gathered, who had persuaded Blaize to look for a holiday house on the Costa Brava. She herself had a villa in the neighbouring town, bought with the divorce settlement her ex-husband had made on her.

She glanced at Katherine's face as she talked. The candle-glow was flattering, concealing the faint lines at the corners of her eyes and mouth, but, even granted that aid, she was a strikingly attractive woman. A smooth, tall, tanned woman with soft hazel eyes and a honeyed voice, who used her long, cool fingers to touch the people she spoke to, creating an air of confidential intimacy.

A good match for Blaize Oliver. A poised, sensual woman who had enough sexuality to keep him interested in bed, and enough intelligence to keep him amused out of it. Maybe she even had what it took to slow down Blaize's consumption of more casual affairs.

They'd been close tonight, with a good deal of laughter, and a good deal of intimate teasing that wasn't open to anyone else in the company.

Yet she was almost certain that they were not physical lovers. There wasn't that feeling between them. It was more the flirty tension of people who were strongly attracted to each other, but who hadn't yet made that initial move. Hadn't made it, but were waiting to make it when the time was right.

Towards Leila herself, his manner had so far been cool and detached. There had been none of the swift attempts at seduction she had expected.

During working hours, especially, he was just short of icy towards her. He hadn't been joking when he'd said he made heavy demands on his staff. He treated her with something less than the consideration he would give to a machine, his manner colder than businesslike. As he gave dictation, or instructed her in work he wanted done, she sometimes got the feeling that he wasn't aware of her presence at all. She was just another machine to him.

Out of working hours, at least, he was slightly more human. For some reason, she often felt that he was laughing at her, but, so far, what it was about her that amused him eluded her. Maybe he thought her naïve, or priggish, after her blushing reaction to his invitation to remove her bikini top. No doubt he found her very unsophisticated compared to a woman like Katherine...

Blaize's affair with Katherine would be a thing of costly gifts and delicate sentiments, leading, ideally, to the chime of wedding bells, the second time around for both of them. And little Tracey would have her wish.

Katherine reached out now, to touch Leila's arm, breaking her line of thought. 'You must have been an exquisite child, Leila, with that golden hair and those big blue eyes. I'm sure your parents spoiled you to bits.'

'I'm afraid they didn't,' Leila replied, trying to make it sound relaxed.

Blaize, sitting near her in the soft darkness, turned his head towards her. 'Were they strict with you?'

'No,' she replied, and picked up her drink. 'They weren't strict, either.'

'What were they, then?' Katherine smiled.

'They weren't anything,' Leila said, 'because they weren't there.'

There was a little silence in their group for a moment, with only the quiet voices of Rick Watermeyer and the others murmuring from the other side of the terrace. Leila cursed herself for having released that bit of personal information. But it was too late to take it back at this stage, and the inevitable sympathetic enquiries would now begin.

'What happened to them?' Blaize asked quietly.

'I don't know,' Leila said lightly. 'I never knew them. They left me when I was a baby, and I don't really even know who they were.'

Katherine breathed a little 'oh' of pity. 'You were abandoned, just like Blaize!'

Leila looked at Blaize's candle-lit face in quick surprise. 'Didn't you have any parents, either?' she couldn't stop herself from asking.

'I had parents, just as you did,' he replied with husky irony. 'We all have parents, Leila. But, like yours, mine weren't too keen on parenthood. Where were you brought up?'

'In care.'

'So was I.' For a moment, they stared at each other. His eyes glinted in the shadow. 'I should have guessed,' he said softly.

So they were alike, then! And all this wealth had been made by Blaize, single-handed. She knew that, in this moment, her feelings towards him had changed. Not that she condoned what she saw as his bad behaviour, but there was a link between them that went deep, something that made them close, whether they accepted that or not.

'But you've got a surname.' Katherine's soft voice intruded into the moment. 'Is that just made-up?'

Leila didn't wince. She'd been asked that before. 'No, it's not made-up,' she replied coolly. 'Thomas was my mother's surname. She had me christened Leila, too.'

'Then you've got birth certificates and so on?' Katherine pursued.

'Yes.'

'Where were you born?'

'In Nottingham. That's where I grew up.'

'Well, if you know all that, you could surely trace at least your mother?' Katherine said brightly. 'I mean, with records, you could almost certainly find out who she is and what she's doing now, and she might even be able to tell you where your father is, too!'

'Yes,' Leila said heavily. 'I probably could do all that.'

'Well, don't you want to?' Katherine demanded, with sublime lack of tact. 'I couldn't *bear* not knowing who my parents were!'

Blaize's voice was wry. 'Maybe Leila's figured that, if her mother didn't want her when she was a baby, she probably wouldn't want her now, either.'

'But people change,' Katherine Henessey protested. 'The poor woman is probably tormented with guilt about what she did, all those years ago. My heart bleeds for her! To give up a child is a terrible thing. Haven't you ever thought of that?'

'Yes,' Leila said, keeping her voice steady with an effort, and fighting down the pain. 'I've thought of that. Now and then.'

'Then your conscience ought to tell you to trace her,' Katherine said firmly. She laid those cool fingers on Leila's hand for emphasis. 'It's no use nursing a grievance for all these years, Leila. I mean, your mother is probably aching for a reconciliation with you. I read the most touching article recently about a woman who——'

'Katherine,' Blaize said gently, 'you're trampling through Leila's nightmares.'

Katherine looked at him in surprise. 'What?'

'Just leave it,' he said, in the same quiet voice. 'If Leila wanted to find her parents, she would have done so.'

He wasn't offering her any sympathy, and she knew better than to ever offer him any. By this stage, you were beyond sympathy. People who'd grown up as she and Blaize had grown up didn't trade in trite condolences. But there was suddenly something else between them— an understanding. Some kind of unspoken bond that went beyond words. Leila felt an odd movement in her breast, as though her heart had turned over inside her, as though he had somehow reached out to touch her in the warm, Spanish night.

'Well, I was only trying to help,' Katherine said, taking her fingers away from Leila's hand. 'I just thought that, with a little push, Leila might——'

'Leila's been pushed a lot in her life,' he interrupted. 'I think she's probably tired of it by now.'

'Oh! You're making me feel *awful*,' Katherine wailed, putting her hand on Blaize's this time. 'I really don't understand what I've said that was so terrible!'

'Of course you don't,' he agreed. 'You had loving parents who spoiled you. We're different.'

Katherine looked quickly from him to Leila, who was lifting a drink to her mouth, and trying to hide the way her fingers were shaking. 'How, different?'

'We're not nice, caring do-gooders like you.' He smiled. 'We're hard and selfish, out for number one, and we like getting our own way in everything.'

'That's a good description of *you*,' Katherine retorted, 'but I'm sure Leila's not like that at all.' She turned to Leila. 'Whatever I said that was so offensive, I'm sorry, Leila. I suppose you've had a harder life than most people?'

'Well, I don't know what other people's lives are like,' she said with an awkward little laugh. 'Mine was hard in some places, easier in others. I certainly prefer being grown-up. I was bored a lot as a child, and since I started with the agency my life has been a lot more interesting.'

'You must be very good to work for Clarewell's,' Katherine said. 'It's the very best agency there is. So your intellect obviously hasn't suffered.'

'One thing about being on your own is that you learn to rely on yourself at a very early age,' Leila said. 'I have a capacity for hard work, that's all.' She was acutely aware of Blaize's attention fixed on her as she spoke. 'And there's something in what Mr Oliver said just now. I haven't made such an amazing success of my life as he has, but I *am* harder than ordinary people. I recognise that, and it's not a very nice quality. However, it can be a useful one.' She twisted the glass in her hands. 'And you didn't offend me when you said I should go and find my mother. It's just not that easy. There's a question of privacy, you see. However deeply my mother suffered when she left me, she had powerful reasons for doing that, and I feel in my heart that they were the sort of reasons that don't go away with the years.'

'You don't know that.'

'No, I don't. I don't know anything, and it's possibly best that way. Just for one thing, she could well be married to another man by now—someone who knows nothing about me, or my mother's past. If I were to turn up out of the blue, claiming to be her long-lost daughter...'

'Yes, I see,' Katherine said slowly. 'But supposing she isn't?'

'And supposing,' Blaize put in, 'she's the sort of woman that Leila wouldn't want as a mother?'

'I don't understand you two,' Katherine sighed, shaking her head. 'Blaize, did you never try to trace your parents?'

'I once made some efforts in that direction,' he said casually. 'I got as far as finding out why they'd abandoned me, at any rate.'

'Oh, Blaize!' Katherine was excited. 'What *was* the reason?'

'Nothing very original, or very cheerful.' He shrugged, deflecting the topic with easy charm. 'But we were talking about Leila. Were you fostered?'

'Yes,' she said, answering the direct question with an effort. 'When they could find families prepared to have me, I was fostered. Otherwise I stayed at special schools.'

'That sounds horrible,' Katherine murmured compassionately.

'It was all right. When I was seventeen, I joined a secretarial college on a grant, and the local authority started feeling I was safe enough to let go. They kept track of me for a while, until I was self-supporting. They did a good job, and I never felt any resentment towards them, only gratitude.'

'And then?' Blaize prompted.

'After that I worked in Nottingham for two years, and then moved to London. After a year with another firm, I joined Carol Clarewell, and...' She shrugged. 'Here I am.'

Blaize toasted her with his glass. 'Not bad. Given your achievement, I'm glad you think my life is such an amazing success,' he said, with more than a touch of self-mockery in his voice.

'Oh, but it *is*,' Katherine exclaimed loyally. 'Blaize has carved himself an empire out of nothing,' she told Leila. 'He was wheeling and dealing in his teens, and by the age of twenty he was on his way to being a stock-market millionaire. He owns over thirty companies, and nobody even knows how rich he is now!'

'That's success in a very limited form,' Blaize said lazily, watching Leila with shadowy green eyes. 'Making money and buying companies is so easy, it's banal. I get the feeling that Leila has got something in her twenties that I'm still looking for at thirty-eight.'

'I can't think what,' Katherine said tartly. 'With all due respect to Leila, she's hardly in your position!'

'And I'm hardly in hers,' Blaize replied. 'Maybe Leila hasn't made a mountain of money, but then she doesn't have a mountain of problems. And she hasn't made a mountain of mistakes, either.'

'You talk like someone who isn't happy with the way his life has gone,' Katherine scoffed.

'Sometimes I wonder whether I am.' Blaize shrugged, draining his glass.

The pulsing beat of an Elton John record filled the warmth of the night. Rick Watermeyer had put the music centre on, and was dancing cheek to cheek with Lucy, the governess.

'To hell with it,' Blaize smiled, reaching for Katherine's hand. 'To hell with everyone. Let's you and I dance.'

Katherine's clear laugh floated back to Leila as she rose to her long legs and drifted into his arms. Leila watched them dance to the sweet tune. Though Katherine was careful to distance herself from Blaize when they talked, when they danced she gave herself to him utterly. Her soft breasts were pressed against him, her hips moving as close as a shadow to his, and her upturned face laughed up at him, her long brown hair streaming down her back.

Neither of them gave Leila a glance. Leila felt the claws of pain unfold in her heart as the old demon, loneliness, awoke in her. Why wasn't it her up there, dancing with Blaize?

Then a crooked smile tugged at her mouth. What? she asked herself bitterly. Had she really imagined there was something between them tonight? Just because it turned out they were both brought up in care?

Think again! Blaize Oliver had risen from humble origins to carve himself an empire—an empire in which Leila was a very small pawn.

His whole career had been mapped out for wealth and stability, right down to the elegant Katherine, who was undoubtedly soon to be his second wife. So what could he ever want with Leila, who came from the kind of background he had been escaping from all his life? Only the satisfaction of another quick conquest. Nothing more.

She wasn't in the same league as Katherine Henessey. She wasn't even a guest here; she was a temporary member of the staff. Anything else was a fantasy she just couldn't afford to indulge in. Men like Blaize didn't dance with the staff. They might tumble them into bed for an hour of knee-trembling fun, if they felt the inclination, but it didn't go further than that.

A servant had materialised at her side, offering another drink. Leila nodded her thanks and took it. She lay back in the chair, and stared up at the stars.

The big house loomed comfortingly behind them, windows glowing like jewels. She thought about what she'd learned tonight. So Blaize had started with nothing, after all. She knew that Katherine hadn't exaggerated about his wealth. In the past two days of taking calls and handling his correspondence, she'd gained a glimpse of real success. A conglomeration of companies, some welded into corporations with their own subsidiaries, others out on a limb in isolated sectors, all having the common denominator that one man, Blaize Oliver, owned them and controlled them.

What on earth could he possibly have meant by saying that she had something he didn't? She had nothing, and he had it all. Looks, charisma, success, happiness.

She looked across at Blaize. He was holding Katherine close, his mouth next to her ear, murmuring something tenderly. Yes, Blaize was something special. Something very special indeed.

I hope you can keep him, she told Katherine silently, watching their embrace turn into a kiss. I hope you mean the love you show his children.

CHAPTER THREE

AS USUAL, the next afternoon was spent by the poolside, working through the 'essential maintenance' letters and calls that had to be done, even during Blaize's holiday.

Leila was starting to sense, rather than actually see, a certain bitterness in Blaize towards the responsibilities dictated by his success. A bitterness that had a great deal to do with the way business interfered with his family life.

Despite what Tracey had told her, there was evidently a strong bond between Blaize Oliver and both of his children. Whatever his morals about other women, he was certainly not an indifferent father, and there was no doubt that he resented anything coming between him and his kids—even the process of making money. But he was also a strict father—almost too strict, in Leila's view. He insisted on both Terry and Tracey keeping up with their schoolwork, and, as she had already seen, he certainly did not believe in spoiling them with money.

When Tracey came down to the poolside to ask for three thousand pesetas, about fifteen pounds, in order to buy a new pair of sun-glasses, she was sent away with a flea in her ear.

'She's got two pairs of sun-glasses already,' Blaize grumbled to Leila as Tracey went disconsolately back to the house. 'What is she, a movie star?'

'Fashion means a lot to young girls.' Leila smiled.

'And money evidently means nothing.'

'You're rather hard on her,' Leila said gently. 'It's not easy for either of them without . . .'

'Without their mother?' Blaize supplied as she hesitated. 'Maybe. But you and I survived without either a mother or a father.'

She dropped her eyes. 'If I were ever to have children, I don't think I'd want them to grow up like me.'

Blaize turned sharply, so that he could look into her eyes. 'Why? What's wrong with you?'

'I didn't say there was anything wrong with me,' she replied, tingling at his intense gaze. 'But just because I had a hard childhood, it doesn't mean that my kids should have to go through that, too!'

'Tracey and Terry have everything,' he rasped, getting up. 'They've got a damned sight too much, in fact.'

Leila thought of the taut, painted nymphet who'd met her at the airport. If he only knew! 'Have they?'

'"Have they?"' he mimicked cruelly. 'What are you looking so knowing about, Miss Thomas? Are you a child psychologist, in addition to all your other accomplishments?'

'No, of course not.'

'Then why the face?'

'I'm not making any faces,' she said formally. 'Your family life is none of my business whatsoever, Mr Oliver. I'm sorry I said anything. Do you want me to finish this letter?'

'Yes. I'm taking a quick swim.' She just caught a glimpse of a muscular back as he dived cleanly into the water. As she watched, he slipped into that easy, cruising beat across the pool, powerful arms swinging in a rhythm of power.

Leila shrugged mentally. What had made her pass any comment about his family? She'd deserved that snub. You just bite your tongue in future, she told herself firmly.

She finished the letter off while he swam, and was waiting patiently as he pulled himself out of the pool again, dripping.

She could not help her eyes from widening to take in the hard, mature body, with its perfect, athletic lines, now glistening with water from his swim. It was the body of a hunter, quintessentially male, lithe and muscular. The black swimming-trunks emphasised, rather than concealed, his masculinity. He had superb thighs, hard and lean, and a stomach that was rippled with strength.

'What are you staring at?' he enquired, reaching for the towel.

'N-nothing,' Leila stammered, her face suddenly hot.

He looked amused. 'Nothing? That isn't very flattering.' He sat down beside her, green eyes dancing with mockery. 'Next letter. This one's to Daniel Matthews, Chairman of Matthews Industries, in Seattle. Ready?'

'I'm ready,' Leila said, blessedly relieved to be getting down to some work.

'Dear Dan,' he started, speaking slowly and easily. 'It was good to see you in Paris last weekend. I enjoyed feeling like a twenty-year-old again. I've been thinking over your suggestion of a merger between your Consolidated Paper Group and my AGP Stationers, and I find the idea has distinct potential.' He inspected the contents of the vacuum-pot. 'Want a cup of coffee, Leila?'

'I'm fine, thank you.'

'OK. It is a possibility which I myself have considered more than once during the recent period of intense economic activity in this particular sector. I'm sending you the relevant trading figures, as I agreed to do, and I'm sure I don't have to remind you again how confidential they are.'

He paused, watching her thoughtfully as he gathered his thoughts. Then he rose, and moved casually round the back of Leila's chair. 'This sun is going to burn your beautiful white skin. Better get some sun-tan lotion on before you blister.'

She started as she felt the drip of oil on her shoulders, and felt powerful, gentle hands start to spread the lotion across her back.

'Given the relative prominence of the parent companies, any information of this kind has high market value,' he went on, before she had a moment to protest. 'I am sending you this material as an act of faith, and I expect the contents to remain at the highest executive level.'

She was tight with reaction as the massaging fingers spread around her neck, their caress exploding her much-vaunted concentration to the point where her pencil had started to shake.

'Mr Oliver——' she began, but he cut through as though she hadn't spoken.

'The prospect of a merger like this is always interesting. Correction. Make that *very* interesting.' Her pencil scratched the addition, then hovered over the paper as if it had a life of its own. More oil trickled on to her skin, and the expert hands smoothed it around her throat, and over the delicate arch of her collarbone, where a pulse was now thudding unsteadily. 'Very interesting. The potential for mutual benefit is extremely high, especially as our two subsidiaries seem so well-suited to a union. Of course,' he said, his voice touched with huskiness as his palms smoothed the initial swell of her breasts, 'there must be a certain introductory period of mutual acquaintance. We have to exchange information at the fullest level, to optimise our later relationship.'

Leila was trembling now, her nerve-endings quivering under his touch. And, hot as the sun was, it was not responsible for the prickle of perspiration that she could feel crawling across her skin. It was practically impossible to keep writing. Why in heaven's name wasn't she doing anything to stop this invasion of her sensitivity?

She seemed to be hypnotised by his presence and his touch, her will fatally weak.

Blaize Oliver moved round to sit beside her again, a symphony of tanned muscle. The green eyes contained something other than amusement now, something darker and more disturbing, as his fingers traced a smooth path from the pulsing base of her throat to the valley between her breasts, caressing in gentle, circular movements.

'I feel certain,' he said softly, staring into her eyes, 'that such an exchange of information can only be beneficial. Trust is essential if we are both to get the most from a merger, and there should be no holding back in any area. Got that?'

'Yes, but I'd rather——'

'What I am talking about,' she heard his voice go on softly, 'is contact at the fullest level, with no reserve of any kind. If we both contract ourselves to full honesty with the other, I feel sure that this could be the most exciting combination of resources we are likely to see this year, and possibly for many years to come.'

His hands were moulding the delicate muscles at the side of her neck, his touch possessive and desirous. 'I know you will appreciate my frankness when I say that I am eager, more than eager, to get the categories in question into an opening approach phase without delay.'

He leaned close to her, as if to check her notes, so close that she could smell his warm, male skin, then studied her mouth with intense green eyes.

'I am working on the assumption, of course, that your division shares your feelings on this matter entirely, and that there will be no opposition at senior managerial, or any other level.'

His hands were at the back of her neck, drawing her to him. She felt his mouth close over hers.

Her own hands had found his shoulders unbidden, their delicate touch exploring his hot, smooth skin. She'd wondered what that mouth would feel like; it felt unashamedly delicious, conquering her with skilled smoothness, his tongue tracing the line of her lips in an agonisingly slow prelude to invasion.

Distantly, she was aware of the pad and pencil slipping to the grass. His palms were massaging her shoulders, smoothing the sheen of oil across them, and Leila could not stop her body from melting helplessly as he plundered her mouth with expert kisses.

Oh, yes, he was an expert, all right. His mouth was cruelly sexual, making her whimper in her throat as electric shocks spread through her stomach. The pull on her aroused senses was frightening, like the hidden potency of an underwater riptide.

He's dangerous! her mind screamed at her. Haven't you been warned about this? This is no game! He'll drown you like the sea, or scorch you like the sun!

She pulled away, panting for breath, her blue eyes dazed with shock. With as much briskness as she could muster, she pushed him away as hard as her strength would allow. Her soul was still trembling like a trapped moth in his hands, but she made a supreme effort to control herself.

'Something wrong?' he asked lazily, still very close to her.

'Mr Oliver,' she said in a shaky voice, 'I'm not going to slap your face for two reasons. One is that you are a very attractive man, and no doubt you've grown used to easy conquests by the poolside, which has made you forget your manners.' She tried to steady her breathing. 'The other is that I'm sure you'd love me to do exactly that, so you can retaliate in kind.' She met his amused eyes coldly. 'But I want you to understand one thing. If you ever attempt to interfere with me again, either in working hours or outside, I'm going to get the next flight back to London.'

'And what will you tell the redoubtable Carol Clarewell when you arrive?' he asked softly.

'That, highly trained as I am, my duties don't include being pawed by my employers.' Leila picked up the pad and pencil. 'I mean what I say, Mr Oliver,' she said, her voice gaining strength. 'I'm not the sort of woman who plays devious games with men. If I felt like a casual affair with you, I wouldn't have stopped you just now.'

'An affair?' he echoed wickedly. 'You think my plans went as far as an affair?'

'However far your plans went, they went a lot too far for me.' She took a deep breath, feeling the oxygen nourish her drugged blood, and started writing. '"I am working on the assumption, of course, that your division shares your feelings on this matter entirely, and that there will be no opposition at senior managerial, or any other level." Have I got that right?'

He leaned back in his chair and laughed softly, his beautiful white teeth framed by tanned lips. 'Do you know something?' he said, his eyes dancing. 'Carol Clarewell was right. You really are something special, Miss Leila Thomas.'

She didn't answer his smile. She disliked him far too much for that. Her voice was dry. 'Resources have to be managed, Mr Oliver, including human resources. I don't have to teach you that, surely? As an extremely efficient secretary, which is what I am, I can be of some value to you. As a bit of slap and tickle beside the pool, I would be totally wasted. I'm sure there are lots of women perfectly eager and willing to fill that role for you.'

'But supposing I like mixing my business with my pleasure?' he smiled, drawing one finger gently down the nape of her neck in a way that awoke goose-bumps across her spine.

'Then find some tart from the local village,' Leila snapped, pulling away from his touch, 'and teach her to take dictation! But don't expect me to learn the kind of morals that prevail in this house!'

'I don't think of you as a tart, Leila.' His voice was gentle. 'As a matter of fact, I find you delicious.'

'Like the oysters we had at lunchtime? I'm not edible, Mr Oliver.'

'I wouldn't count on that,' he warned silkily. His near-naked body was so close to hers, his power so over-whelmingly impending, that she moved away instinc-tively. 'You're really angry, aren't you? It wasn't my intention to offend you just now, and I'm sorry if I did.'

'What else could an approach like that be, but of-fensive?' she demanded shortly.

'You didn't seem to mind,' he pointed out, green eyes holding hers. 'In fact, you seemed to be enjoying it as much as I was.'

Leila looked down hotly. Two hard peaks in the thin material of her top bore out his allegation. 'No, Mr Oliver,' she said tightly, 'I was not enjoying myself. Do you want to add any more to this letter, or was it all just a fantasy to distract my attention?'

'Well, well,' he said softly, watching her from under those thick dark lashes. 'You *are* something special.'

'I'm just one of the rare ones who doesn't collapse in the first round,' she said drily.

'What about the second round?' he enquired smoothly. 'Or the third?'

'There will be no second or third rounds,' she re-minded him sharply. 'Not unless you want to find yourself sitting here alone tomorrow, waiting for my re-placement. Perhaps your oh, so subtle approach will work better with her!'

He was amused. 'You think I try this with every sec-retary who comes to work for me?'

'Oh, I'm quite certain that this is the standard test,' Leila retorted. 'And I'm equally certain that it usually works. I just hope you have the intelligence to accept the rare occasions when it doesn't.'

Blaize grinned. 'Do I strike you as the kind of man who gives up easily?' he asked

'If that's your attitude——' She rose quickly to her feet, and reached for her robe. 'You'd better ring for another temp, Mr Oliver. We're just wasting each other's time here. There's a flight back to London tonight, and I'm sure I can still get a seat on it——'

'No.' He rose to confront her, tall and muscular. The laughter had gone from his eyes. 'No,' he repeated quietly, his hands closing round her slim arms, imprisoning her. 'Don't be absurd, Leila. I want you here.'

'Then let me go,' she said coldly. 'I won't be manhandled, Mr Oliver.'

His face tightened, but, with an effort, he obeyed her. 'Touch me not, is that it?'

'Touch me not,' she agreed, her expression icy. She met his gaze, her eyes discs of cool aquamarine, fringed with golden-brown lashes. 'I've been touched once too often in my life, Mr Oliver. I've learned that I don't have to be touched if I don't want it. I hope you understand that. Now, do you want to move on to the next letter?'

He stared at her tautly, his eyes narrowed. Suddenly one, and then the other, of the two telephones began to ring. The moment was broken.

'You take that one,' he said quietly, and they both reached out to pick up the insistent telephones.

Leila felt less than up to par on Tuesday morning. Whether it was the sunburn or the change of diet and climate—or the restless dreams that had made her sleep a torment for the past week—she was headachey and bad-tempered. It was a great relief that she would be in the office this morning, working with the word processor, instead of being cooked by the pool. Blaize was flying with Rick this morning, and had left her in peace, with a heap of letters to send.

Over-sensitive shoulders forced her to pick the bright sun-dress again, which was both cool and strapless. She breakfasted lightly with Lucy and the children, said little to anyone, and took her coffee straight up to the office.

It was in the huge attic of the main house, and equipped as a full-scale operations centre, with all the communications and computer equipment necessary to keep Blaize in touch with his empire. The skylit room was spotlessly clean and orderly, with everything in a logical place, and everything to hand where it was needed. The kind of environment she worked best in.

She slipped easily into the mechanical routine of typing up correspondence and taking calls, her mind dealing comfortably with seven different things at once.

Katherine Henessey was coming round for drinks and dinner tonight. Leila found herself wondering bitterly whether Blaize would ever give Katherine the brutally direct approach he'd used with her at the poolside the other day. Unlikely, she decided. That was for inferiors like herself.

Suddenly the memory of his kiss was tinglingly alive on her full lips. Was that the way he had propositioned those last two temps?

Did he always start like that, an approach refined over the years to produce the maximum effect as quickly as possible?

Leila reached for another heap of notes, trying not to think about it any more. There had been no further attempt to woo her, anyway. For that, at least, she ought to be grateful.

At eleven, Pedro the gardener-chauffeur arrived to take the post into the village. She told him which ones were for express delivery, and then took a few moments' break to make herself a cup of coffee before launching back into her tasks.

At noon, Blaize arrived back from his flying lesson.

Wearing a well-used leather jacket and jeans, he looked a long way from the popular image of a millionaire. It was only when you met his eyes, and saw the hard purpose there, that you knew he could never have been a poor man.

His presence was devastatingly male as he perched on her desk and flipped through the copies of the letters she'd sent that morning.

'Your calls are on your desk,' she told him. 'Some of them sound very urgent.'

'Everything's very urgent,' he commented drily. 'I only deal with the desperate stuff.' His lean fingers riffled through the sheaf of flimsies. 'Hmm. You've been a busy little bee.' He drew out one particularly long letter and studied it. She'd had to type it up from a collection of laconic notes and near-incomprehensible scribblings he'd left her, some of them on the back of one of Rick Watermeyer's cigarette packs. She waited with some trepidation as he checked it over. But his expression, if he wore one, was satisfied. 'You're not bad, are you?'

'It's all a question of neatness,' she told him. 'I was always a neat little girl.'

Vivid green eyes looked down at her from a bronzed face framed by thick dark hair. 'Yeah,' he grunted. 'I was a neat little boy, and all. All those strange beds, where you had to turn the sheets down to the millimetre. All those strange tables, where you had to leave your knife and fork just so.'

'All those strange rooms,' she couldn't stop herself from echoing, 'where there were your things, and other children's things.'

'And never the twain shall meet.' He dropped the correspondence back in the tray. He turned to her. 'You *did* trace your mother, didn't you?' The sudden question was asked with a green stare that went straight to the back of her skull. 'You were lying to Katherine the other night.'

Leila felt the colour rise to her face, hot and unbecoming. 'That's *my* business!' she snapped back.

'What did you find out?' he asked relentlessly, holding her eyes. 'Anything that helped you to explain your existence on this planet, cool Miss Thomas?'

'You have no right to ask me——'

'Was she as beautiful as you are?'

'Stop!'

'Or did you just get a nasty shock, something that froze your heart, and turned you into the frigid little pink of prudery you now are?'

'Leave me alone!' she said fiercely, rising to face him. 'Just leave me alone, Mr Oliver. I don't want to share any part of my life with you——'

'Was she pleased to see you?' He was remorseless, his fingers biting into her shoulders to stop her from turning away. 'Did she welcome you with open arms, Leila? Was there a touching scene between the long-lost daughter and her errant mum?'

'You know damned well there wasn't!' As though something had broken inside her, Leila felt tears fill her eyes. 'There was no touching scene, and there was no mum. What the hell do you keep asking for?'

'Because I want to know,' he said roughly. 'Because you and I are the same inside.'

'We're not!'

'Yes, we are.' He was so close to her, his proximity dominating her senses. 'Tell me what happened, Leila.'

'Nothing happened.' She clenched her fists as the images rose up in her mind, the wounds as fresh and sharp as if it had been yesterday, instead of over five years ago. 'There was nothing that could happen.'

'You traced her? You found out who she was?'

'Yes,' Leila nodded wearily, her eyes blurred with the tears that still hadn't spilled. 'Yes, I found out exactly who she was.'

His fingers eased on her shoulders, moving down her back to support, rather than restrain her. 'Was it difficult?' he asked, his voice gentler.

'No. It took some time, but it wasn't difficult. She was still living in Nottingham, a few miles from where I was at college.'

'How old were you?'

'Eighteen.'

'Tell me what happened,' he commanded huskily. 'You've got to tell someone, some time, so it might as well be someone who can understand, Leila.'

His closeness dazed her, somehow forcing the words out of her heart. 'I—I'd made absolutely certain that I had the right woman,' she said, her voice sticking in her throat. 'I knew it was her. There weren't any doubts about it. The moment I saw her, I knew I was right...'

'She looked like you?'

'Taller, but the same hair and eyes. Even the same face. She was very smart. She ran a big dry-cleaning agency in the high street.'

'Married?'

Leila swallowed the aching lump in her throat. 'Yes.' She nodded. 'She was married. No children. Not—not married to my father, of course.'

'Of course not,' he said drily.

'It took me a long, long time to work up the courage to face her. At first I couldn't even think of a way to get close to her. Then, in the end, I wrote her a letter.'

'What kind of letter?' Blaize asked, his eyes narrowed. 'Not some mawkish screed, blotted with tears and sentiment?'

'Of course not,' Leila told him tiredly. 'Just a note, really. I sent it to the agency, asking her to meet me in a restaurant, nothing more. I signed my name, and hoped she'd come.'

'And did she?'

'Yes, she came.'

His arms drew her close, overcoming her resistance, until she was cradled against his broad, hard chest, his arms holding her slim shoulders. 'And?'

'And we talked. Just talked, like acquaintances who hadn't met for a few years. She asked me about my life, what I'd done, what my plans were. And told me a little about herself. How happily married she was, how her husband was a very successful businessman, on the local council, about her job, and how happy it made her...'

His strong muscles tensed around her, protective and defensive. 'Did she acknowledge being your real mother?'

Leila was silent for a moment. At last, she went on in a low voice, 'Right at the end, I told her how I'd traced the records to her. She listened politely. I just wanted to hear her say it, Blaize. I didn't want anything from her, heaven knows! I didn't want money or attention, or even love. I would have walked out of there and been content never to have seen her again. I just wanted to hear her say that she was my mother! B-but she wouldn't. She looked me in the eyes, and she said, "Oh, no. You must be mistaken, my dear. I've never had any children. My husband can't have any."'

'Did you try and press her?' he asked quietly.

'It wasn't any use. She said she had a good job, and lots of money, and a lovely home, and a wonderful husband. And that was all. She said—she said she was sure my real mother must be dead. She told me to stop looking for her, and wished me luck with my life. Then she paid the bill, and walked out of there. I never even got a chance to ask her about my father.'

She'd been almost unaware that she was clinging to Blaize, as though for comfort. Tired of fighting him, and her memories, she sagged in his arms and rested her cheek against her chest. The steady thud of his heart was against her temple, the leather smell of his jacket male and comforting. When she closed her eyes her long lashes spilled the hot tears down her cheeks. Blaize stroked her hair gently, waiting for her to get control of her emotions.

At last she looked up at him, her mouth quivering. 'Well?' she asked. 'Are you satisfied now?'

'At least it's got you into my arms,' he replied in a satisfied rumble. 'I've been wondering how to do this for the past week.'

'Is that all you care about?' she gasped, starting to draw away. His iron-hard muscles held her.

'What else is there to care about?' he demanded, drinking in the wet, aquamarine depths of her eyes. 'You're lovely when you cry, Leila. Tears are a great aid to seduction, did you know that?' He smiled wickedly, imprisoning her. 'Get them to cry a little, and you're half-way there.'

'I hate you,' she choked, struggling.

'Of course you don't,' he purred. 'Stop fighting your natural inclinations. We got off to a bad start, Leila——'

'And is this any better?' she challenged angrily.

'It feels better to me. You're so beautiful...' He bent to kiss her throat.

When he'd kissed her before, it had been with deliberate sensuality, full on the lips. This was different. His mouth was incredibly gentle now, offering a consolation that was both treacherous and intoxicating. Her resistance had nothing to grasp at as his velvety mouth moved over her face, kissing her cheeks, her eyelids, the scented skin of her temples, anywhere but the soft lips that were parting helplessly for him.

With wicked astuteness, he had been right. Getting her to remember all that past grief had softened her opposition, making her all too helpless in his arms. She wanted the comfort he could give her, illusory though it was...

It took only the slightest movement to bring her mouth into contact with Blaize's, but Leila knew that the movement had been hers, and that this time she had wanted the kiss.

His mouth was warm and firm. A meltingly sweet response unfolded in her, drawing her irresistibly to him. Her mouth opened under his pressure, and their kiss deepened to an intimate contact of tongues.

The world stopped turning around them. Pain was stilled in her. Nothing was real any more, but the touch of this man. His hands were caressing downwards, moulding the curves of her body beneath the light material of her sun-dress, holding her breasts in the cups of his palms, his thumbs finding the peaks of desire at their centres.

She arched to him with a little moan of hunger.

She knew exactly how expertly she'd been deceived, but it didn't matter. That was the cruel cleverness of him; right now, she didn't care that he was a cold-blooded womaniser, a man whose morals she could never respect. What mattered was the feeling that he understood her. She'd told him something she'd never told another human being, and had seen the miracle of understanding in his eyes—understanding that was worth more than an ocean of pity to her right now.

'How have we lasted this long?' he groaned, crushing her in his arms. 'Why do you keep me at arm's length, Leila? You're not a virgin, are you? You know how good we'd be together!'

'You're too good with too many women,' she whispered, her hands pale and slender as they caressed the bronzed column of his neck. 'That's your trouble! I told you once before, I'm not the kind of girl who has casual affairs!'

'Who says it's going to be casual?' he purred.

'*Any* kind of affairs,' she amended.

'In which case, what are you doing in my arms?'

'Spilling my heart out to you,' Leila said ruefully. 'Spilling my very unwise heart out to someone who's an expert at getting women's secrets, but who doesn't really give a damn about them.'

His thumb traced the full curve of her lower lip gently, his eyes studying it as though he was imagining how it would feel, touching other parts of his body. 'Come on, gorgeous. You're not a sentimental idiot at this stage of your life, surely?'

'I'm not any kind of idiot.' Again, she tried hard to get away, but he was so strong. 'You said you wouldn't try anything like this again!'

'But the game has many rules.' He grinned.

'It's *not* a game!' She was starting to get really angry. 'You're an unscrupulous bastard, Blaize. You'll do anything to get your way——'

'I'll do anything to get my way with *you*,' he said roughly. His palms stroked down the taut line of her waist, following the curve of her hips and thighs, drawing her close against him. 'I want you, Leila. You don't have a hope of resisting, do you know that?'

This time he gave her no option about kissing him. Their mouths closed again, the excitement turning into flame, leaping along her veins. She tried to fight away, knowing it was madness.

Then they both heard the door open, and Leila turned quickly as Blaize's arms released her.

Oh, no! Her rescuer was the last person she wanted to see right now.

She met Tracey Oliver's widening green eyes. There was a stretched silence. Then Blaize asked sharply, 'What is it, Tracey?'

The colour had drained from the girl's face so quickly that Leila thought she was going to faint.

'It's Terry,' she said dully. 'Miss Lucy says she thinks he's got measles.'

'Damn,' Blaize muttered. 'I thought it was just a cold. He was never immunised,' he told Leila, frowning.

'Tracey was, but he missed out. Double damn! I'll have to go and see. Is he in his bed?'

Tracey nodded silently. Blaize touched Leila's cheek as if in mute apology for having to leave her, and went out of the room to see his son.

There wasn't anything she could say to Tracey, so Leila sat down and turned back to the screen of her word processor without a word. Her heart was thudding painfully against her ribs, her whole body weak with the explosive cocktail of emotion and desire he'd awoken in her.

'Your promises don't mean much,' Tracey said bitterly from behind her.

''Do you think not?' Leila said, staring at her own dark reflection in the screen.

'You said you'd stay away from my father!' Tracey accused, coming forward.

'But did you say that your father would stay away from *me*?' Leila retorted, swinging on her chair to face the teenager. 'I'm not making any of the moves, Tracey. You're adult enough to see that!'

'All·I see is that he can't take his eyes or his hands off you,' Tracey hissed fiercely. 'And you do everything in your power to encourage him!'

'That's not true.' She was too emotional to face a quarrel with an undiscerning teenager right now, but she had no option. 'Listen to me,' she said, appealing to the hot-eyed girl for understanding. 'What you saw just now wasn't a tender love-scene. It was something else, something you're still too young to understand.'

'I'm not too young to understand you!'

'I'm afraid you are,' Leila said patiently. 'I don't *want* to get involved with your father. Do you think I'm the sort of person who makes a habit of sleeping with my boss? I'm not. If you knew anything about me, you'd understand that without having to be told!'

'Then why do you let him touch you and kiss you?'

The question, asked with such childlike simplicity, was unanswerable. Leila shook her golden head gently. 'I don't know. But I promise you one thing—I have no intention of getting involved with your father.'

'You don't mean a thing to him!' The youthful voice was so cruel. 'You're just another casual lay to him!'

'That's no way to talk, Tracey,' Leila said shortly.

'That's all you are.' Tracey threw the words at her, her eyes blazing. 'Another affair!'

Leila's mouth tightened. It shocked her to hear this fifteen-year-old girl talking like this, but what could she do? The girl had learned to see the world like that. And Leila's own life had given her too much in common with Tracey for her to feel anything but understanding and pity for the confused child.

And, in any case, she knew in her heart that Tracey was right, so what hypocritical point was there in telling her to stop?

'Can't you see the way things are with him and Katherine?' Tracey was asking tensely. 'She's the only woman who has any chance of making Dad settle down again. But if you start an affair with him under her nose, everything will just fall to pieces. She's so decent, can't you see? She'd be broken-hearted. She'd never forgive him. Katherine's *different* from you,' the girl said in a low voice. 'She cares about my dad, and she cares about us. She's worth a hundred of you!'

Leila met the hostile stare levelly. 'You're going to have to do some fast growing up, Tracey. And start realising that insulting me—or any of the other women who work for your father—is not going to sanitise his character for Katherine Henessey's benefit. Do you understand what I'm saying?' Tracey didn't answer, but she dropped her eyes in front of Leila's clear blue look. 'Katherine is going to have to take your father as she finds him,' Leila went on in a steady voice. 'And so are you, Tracey.

If Katherine doesn't know what he's like by now, then she'll be marrying him under a false impression. He's no angel, and, despite what you think, I don't think she is, either. Honesty is the best policy. You don't want another divorce in your life, do you?'

'Don't say that,' the girl flared at her. 'How *dare* you talk about Katherine like that? You've got no right!'

'Judgements are unpleasant, aren't they?' Leila pointed out. She drew a slow breath. 'Now, your brother sounds as though he's pretty sick. Why don't you forget about me and your father for a while, and go and see if you can help?'

Tracey turned on her heel mutinously. At the doorway, however, she turned to glance back at Leila.

'What were you crying about?' she asked after a moment's silence.

'Myself,' Leila said tiredly. 'Whenever I cry, that's what I always cry about.'

CHAPTER FOUR

TERRY'S measles were confirmed by the doctor, a diagnosis that didn't come as a surprise to everyone who'd seen the blotchy red rash on the boy's skin. He was thoroughly miserable, but determined to be brave about it, his spotty face screwed up with discomfort over the mound of blankets that the doctor ordered. Leila's heart went out to him. She went to see him as often as she could over the week that passed, knowing how much distraction would mean to a nine-year-old cooped up with a nasty illness.

Katherine Henessey, however, was notable by her absence. While quick to express sympathy, she was obviously bored with the sick-bed routine, and had not been a frequent visitor. Leila wondered whether Blaize had noticed this little failing in the normally flawless Katherine.

On Friday evening, she gave a worn-out Lucy a night off, and sat with the boy, reading him stories in his little bedroom while the governess caught up on some much-needed sleep.

Blaize came in two or three times during the evening, sitting in silence on the opposite side of the bed, and watching the boy's face thoughtfully as Leila read.

To give him credit, he had seemed seriously concerned about his son's welfare over this past week. For once, at least, there had been no insistence that Terry should not be spoiled. At times, when it had looked as though Terry's fever might become dangerous, she'd seen Blaize look positively drawn with worry.

Even the hardest men, she decided, must have a weak spot or two. In someone like Blaize, it was usually the children. She respected him all the more for his obvious sincerity of feeling; but it was still rather strange to see the ruthless tycoon turned concerned father.

Terry's temperature was up tonight, and the rash seemed to be reaching its peak. Unable to sleep for the headache and the fever, the boy was grizzly and tearful by eleven-thirty. Blaize, who'd held out all week against giving Terry the sedatives the doctor had left, turned to Leila with a worried frown.

'Should we give him a pill? I hate the thought of giving a child drugs, but he's so wretched...'

'Is there any camomile tea in the house?' Leila asked, smoothing the boy's damp fringe away from his forehead.

'Camomile?' Blaize raised sceptical eyebrows. 'That's an old wives' remedy, surely?'

'It's just what he needs,' Leila said firmly.

With a shrug, Blaize let himself out of the bedroom, and made for the kitchen. He was back in ten minutes, with a large cup of steaming orange tea.

'Josefina, the cook, had some,' he told Leila. 'What about it, Terry? Fancy some nice hot tea?'

Terry whimpered, turning his face away from the cup. Leila propped him up against her breast, cradling him in her arms, and took the tea from Blaize.

Murmuring soothingly to him, she made him sip the camomile, making sure he got a good half of it down. Blaize watched her, his dark brows lowered. But his scowl eased as Terry's weary head started to droop.

Within minutes, the boy was sleeping peacefully in Leila's arms. She held him for ten minutes longer, making sure he was fast asleep, stroking his hot forehead with cool fingers.

When she was sure he was firmly in the land of dreams, she looked up at Blaize. His eyes were on her, deep and brooding. Beyond him, Tracey was standing in the doorway in her nightie, watching her with an expression so oddly like her father's that Leila was startled.

She nodded silently to Blaize to ease the blankets back, then lowered the boy into his bed.

Terry curled on his side with a little whimper, but, after a few sniffles, was fast asleep again, his hands uncurling.

Blaize tucked him in gently. Silently, Tracey slipped away to her own bedroom. Switching the light off, so that only the tiny glow of the night-light remained, Blaize took Leila's arm and led her quietly out of the room.

They went downstairs to the deserted lounge, where Blaize poured them both a whisky.

'That was pretty magical stuff,' he said, dropping ice in the crystal tumblers.

'It's very good,' Leila nodded. 'And it's better than drugs, especially for a sick child.'

'I wasn't talking about the camomile,' Blaize said gently.

Leila smiled as she accepted the whisky. 'You think I worked some kind of spell on Terry?'

'I saw you do it.' He lifted his glass in a silent toast. 'Anyhow, thanks for doing it.'

'I'll take some blankets into his room tonight.' The whisky felt good, easing her tiredness. 'I'll be quite comfortable on the chair.'

'No. You're a honey, but my room's just opposite, and I'm a very light sleeper—especially where the kids are concerned. You get some sleep.'

'It's no trouble to me,' she assured him.

'I don't want you falling asleep over the computer tomorrow,' he said with a touch of dryness. 'But thanks for the offer. You've been very kind to the boy all this week. It wasn't necessary for you to add being a nursemaid to all your other duties.'

'Oh, I love children,' she said lightly. 'It was no hardship to spend a little time with your son.'

He drained the glass at a gulp, then gave her one of those hard, direct stares. 'If you love kids so much, why don't you get married and have a few of your own?'

'I might, some day.'

'Not if you keep gallivanting round the world for Carol Clarewell,' he said, pouring himself a second drink. 'How will you ever meet the right sort of man? You're going to wake up one morning and find that you've turned into one of those efficient office spinsters who never get married at all.'

'Is that such a terrible fate?' Leila asked lightly.

'For you, yes,' he said, eyes on hers. 'You were born for love and motherhood.'

Squirming away from the topic, Leila asked, 'Are you going to tell his mother that he's got measles?'

'His mother doesn't give a twopenny damn about him,' Blaize growled. 'Nor about Tracey.'

'That's a hard thing to say,' she protested.

'I could say harder things if I were to have another couple of whiskies,' he retorted. 'The boy, frankly, was a mistake. I should have been warned by Vanessa's reaction to Tracey. She was never a mother to the poor kid. She could never be bothered. After Terry came along, she just couldn't wait to get out of the house quick enough each morning. That was when I really started seeing through my beloved wife's character,' he added acidly. 'No, Leila, I'm not going to tell Vanessa that Terry has measles. She hasn't seen him for thirteen months, and she hasn't seen Tracey for nearly two years. Do you think a few spots are going to bring her running now?'

She'd underestimated the bitterness that lay within Blaize. It was glittering now in the deep green eyes, curling the passionate mouth into a curve of contempt.

'Perhaps things will change as the children get older,' she suggested hesitantly.

'Oh, come on,' he snorted. 'You and I both know very well that some women just aren't suited to mother-hood. Probably something in the hormones. Most of them make some kind of effort, out of a sense of duty, or because of social pressures. But there are some mothers who have about as much mother-love as a female jellyfish.'

He offered her the whisky bottle, but she shook her head. He didn't pour himself a third, but capped the bottle and put it down. He was very controlled in his drinking, she'd noticed, and didn't smoke.

'As for au pairs and governesses and nannies,' he went on, 'Lucy is just the latest in a long line. They aren't the answer, either. None of them has the necessary com-mitment, and you can't blame them. The kids fall out with them, and the next thing you know they're heading back to their agencies. No,' he said, rising and walking to the window, 'if Tracey and Terry are ever to have a mother in their lives again, I'll have to marry someone else—someone with enough room in her heart to take them in.'

Leila looked up at him quickly. She wouldn't nor-mally have dreamed of saying anything, but the memory of Tracey's bitter green eyes rose up in her mind, prompting her to speak. 'Well,' she ventured, 'there seems to be a likely candidate in the offing...'

'You mean Kate?' he said, looking out at the night.

'I think your daughter approves of her, if that's any-thing to go by,' Leila said delicately.

'I know all about Tracey's opinions on Kate,' he re-plied brusquely. 'She tends to make herself rather a nuisance about it.'

Leila wondered whether Blaize had any idea just how far his daughter was prepared to go in her defence of Katherine Henessey's candidature as surrogate mother. 'You've just said that she hasn't ever had a proper mother,' she pointed out, her lingering sense of guilt towards the girl making her unwisely forward. 'And Katherine does seem very fond of them both.'

'So those pretty blue eyes are sharp little watchers, after all,' he said, rather grimly. 'You're doing the child psychologist routine again, are you?'

'No, and I don't want to trespass,' Leila said, recognising a snub when she got one. She rose to her feet. 'Well, I'll get off to bed, if I'm not wanted any more...'

'I'm not the marrying kind, Leila.' He turned to face her, hard-eyed. 'I wasn't the marrying kind even *before* Vanessa. If I were ever to consider changing my mind, then, yes—Katherine Henessey would be the first woman I'd ask.'

'Ah,' Leila said quietly. Tracey would have jumped for joy if she'd heard that, but, for some reason, a cold fist had just squeezed Leila's heart. She forced herself to go on. 'It seems to me that Katherine has a lot more to offer than just a mother-figure for your children.'

'Oh, yes,' Blaize agreed lazily, 'she's sexy, intelligent and stylish into the bargain. I enjoy her company as much as any woman's I've ever been with. She's got the poise to cope with the kind of chaos that usually prevails in my life. But I'd still have only one reason for marrying,' he concluded brusquely. 'And that would be to give the kids a mother. I don't want a wife, Leila. I don't want one, and I don't need one.'

'Then you shouldn't even be considering marriage,' Leila said, shocked at his callous approach.

'Who says I am considering it? I can do without that kind of restriction in my life.'

'Yes, I can see that,' Leila said drily. 'Well, Mr Oliver, none of our parents made much of a sacrifice for us. So why should you make a sacrifice for *your* kids?'

Her irony made his face darken angrily. The tanned arms were hard with muscle as he put his hands on his hips. 'I love Terry and Tracey. But tying myself to one woman, even for their sake, would be a bad mistake, Leila.'

'The rest of the world seems to get along with that system,' she couldn't help needling him.

'The rest of the world lies and cheats,' he retorted. 'Ever read the latest statistics on marriage and divorce, baby blue eyes? Modern marriage is a long catalogue of adultery and betrayal.'

'Not all modern marriages are like that,' she said forcefully.

'No?' he sneered. 'You and I are both illegitimate, Leila. I'm divorced. Rick Watermeyer is separated from his wife. Katherine Henessey is divorced. Even Mrs Saunders, the housekeeper, is divorced. In this household alone, there are seven people whose lives have been affected by infidelity. It's human nature. Accept it, girl!'

'This is a particular household,' Leila said briskly, 'with a particular class of people in it. Rich, well-educated, and spoiled. People in that category have a very high incidence of divorce, yes. That doesn't mean that the whole institution of marriage is disintegrating.'

'Well, cherish your illusions if they keep you warm at night,' he said drily. 'The fact is that there's no biological pressure on adults to stay faithful. In fact, their biology points them in exactly the opposite direction. But there *is* a biological necessity for children to have a mother.'

'Which means you've got a problem,' she said sweetly, 'doesn't it?'

'Yes, I have a problem,' he replied silkily. 'My problem is that I'm constitutionally unable to trust women. Even paragons of virtue like Kate Henessey.'

Leila gave him a smile touched with bitterness. 'Really? That explains a lot of things about you.'

'Exactly.' He nodded. His smile was astringent as he came over to her. He reached out to touch her hair, and she flinched. 'It explains everything.'

'But perhaps it's *you* who's untrustworthy?' she challenged boldly.

'In what way?'

'In that you obviously can't settle down with one woman!'

'I might give it a try,' he glinted, stroking her sensitive neck with the backs of his knuckles. 'With the right woman, one day...'

'For the sake of your children, I hope you do. Can't you see how much they need stability?' She moved away from the gently caressing fingers. 'Can't you understand that they don't just need a mother? They need *you* to settle down in one permanent relationship.'

'When there are such delicious prizes in the world as you to be won?' he said softly. 'That's a hard sentence, Leila.'

'I've been told Katherine Henessey's worth a hundred of me.' The stupid words were out before she had the wit to censor them.

Blaize's eyes narrowed. 'What are you talking about?' he asked shortly.

Leila gulped. 'Oh, nothing. I was talking in general terms.'

'Has Tracey been saying something to you?' he growled. He ripped the truth out of her eyes. 'So she has. That interfering, nosy little—— She's going to find she's not too old to be put over my knee!'

'Please!' Anxiety flooding her at his angry expression, she put her hand on his arm. 'Don't say anything to her, for heaven's sake. She's a very confused, unhappy teenager, and giving her hell for expressing her feelings is the last thing she needs right now!'

'Well, well.' Lean fingers trapped her hand as she pulled it away. 'So you really care about the little brat? That's the first time you've ever touched me voluntarily, do you realise that?' The devastatingly handsome face looked down at her with a slow smile. 'Is that your soft spot, Leila? Other people's children?'

'I happen to feel sorry for yours,' she said, trying not to respond as his fingers trailed up her arm, his caress raising goose-bumps of pleasure all the way.

'Well, don't,' he murmured, pulling her to him despite her resistance. 'Tracey is a lot harder and a lot less helpless than you give her credit for. Why not try feeling sorry for *me*, instead?'

'Oh, I do feel sorry for you, Mr Oliver.' It was an effort to keep her voice cool and impersonal. 'I think you're even more confused and unhappy than your daughter is.'

'Go on,' he smiled, not letting her go. 'As long as you keep talking about me, I reckon there's still a chance...'

'A chance of what?'

'Of carrying through my plans for your seduction.'

'I've had a taste of your technique already!' she snapped, her nerves jumping at his proximity. 'And, quite frankly, I found it crude, Mr Oliver. Crude and unrefined, and therefore utterly unexciting.'

'That was before I'd summed you up properly,' he smiled. 'I was way out of line that afternoon. Making a grab wasn't the right way to go about it, and my only excuse was that I kind of lost control of myself. But I know a lot more about you, now. For example,' he said, his voice lowering to a purr as he drew her close, 'I've discovered that you love to be kissed gently on your eyelids, like this...' His mouth illustrated the point with bone-melting effectiveness. 'And then on your throat and neck, like this...'

Leila's throat arched back, exposing the tender skin to his lips in a momentary response she could not control. Sweetness flooded her veins at his touch.

His kisses were changing from wickedly deliberate expertise to something less controlled. They became urgent, yet never rough, caressing the fine skin of her temples, the yielding sweetness of her mouth, as though he could not get enough of her to adore.

He murmured her name once or twice, revelling in the scent of her skin. Leila's arms were sliding round his neck as his mouth moved downwards, finding the scented valley between her breasts. The buttons of her unpretentious cotton blouse opened under his questing fingertips, revealing the swell of her breasts, cupped in the pale blue lace of her bra.

With a little groan of desire, he kissed the perfumed curves. Dazed, Leila cradled his head, her fair skin so pale against the tanned face of Blaize Oliver. What was she doing, embracing her destruction like this? She had to resist, stop him from giving her any more of this treacherous pleasure!

Yet she felt so weak suddenly, her very movements of protest seeming to melt into a languorous invitation.

'Leila,' he whispered huskily, 'how lovely you are. I don't know how I've managed to keep my hands off you this past week! You have the face of an angel, yet your mouth is made for temptation.'

'Please, no...'

'From the moment I saw you, I've been burning for you.' Her eyes fluttered closed. She felt Blaize's fingers cup her face, turning her mouth to his as though he had every right in the world, as though she belonged to him, body and soul...

His kiss was perfect, taking the soft, clinging surrender of her lips for granted. She held him as though her life depended upon it, as though nothing else were real except Blaize, except the need for her she could feel in him.

His fingertips caressed the naked skin of her arms and back, making her shiver with desire as they trailed up her flanks towards her breasts. The material of her bra was so fine and smooth that it was almost a second skin, making his caress tantalising and frustrating. His fingers told him that her nipples were erect with hunger, and her gasp of pleasure told him exactly what his caress was doing to her.

Her body seemed fused to his, her loins pressed to the hardness of his desire, her thighs against his. Panic rose in her as she felt her response going beyond her control, their kiss growing to become something more than just a moment of sexual pleasure, growing to fill her heart and mind until she thought she would burst.

She pushed him away with all her fast-fading strength.

'No,' she begged him shakily. 'Don't force this on me, Blaize!'

'Force?' he rumbled. 'My darling, the last thing I want is to force you! All I want you to do is face reality for once. Don't you know how much I want you?'

'I—I know that you want to take me to bed——'

'Yes,' he said with a slow smile. 'I want to take you to my bed, Leila, and undress you with great care.'

'Stop!' she whispered.

'I want to kiss every part of your body,' he murmured, drawing her close again. 'I want to taste you, love you with all the skill of which I am capable. I want to see you faint and dizzy with pleasure in my arms!'

'No,' she pleaded, covering her ears with her palms, 'don't say any more!'

He kissed her mouth gently, drawing her protective hands away from her ears as he did so. 'I'm going to have you, Leila. I'm going to make you mine. You know that as well as I do. Perhaps not tonight, or even tomorrow. But soon—the moment I see the look in your eyes that tells me you are ready.'

'Never.' She shook her head numbly. 'Is it your colossal vanity that makes you so deaf? I am *not* one of your offhand conquests.'

'No.' He smiled smokily. 'You're something much more special. But you won't accept the truth about us.'

'I won't accept your version of the truth,' Leila said. She knew that if she did not stop him now, say something cutting enough to turn him aside, she would not be able to resist this sweet torment much longer.

Her hands were trembling as she pulled her collar closed.

'As I said,' she told him, finding a colder voice with a supreme effort, 'your technique is crude and unrefined. Save it for someone less fussy, Mr Oliver. Unlike you, I don't have a pathological need for casual sex. I'm going to bed. *Alone.* Goodnight.'

He jerked her round to face him, the exasperation in his eyes telling her that her verbal needle had struck home somewhere in that usually impenetrable hide.

'You've got a sharp little tongue, Leila. Where did you learn to put men off so efficiently? On one of those mysterious occasions you told me about, when you were touched once too often in your life?'

'That's right,' she rejoined, facing him like a snared hind. 'I also told you that I've learned I don't have to put up with approaches I don't welcome!'

'Who was he?' Blaize demanded. 'Some overweight, over-amorous boss? Some office Romeo who cornered you behind the filing-cabinet?'

'I don't want to talk about it.'

'But *I* do.' He trapped her in his arms. 'I want to hear all about it.'

'It's none of your business!'

'It is if it's coming between us,' he rejoined grimly.

'There's a lot more than *that* coming between us,' Leila retorted. Her eyes were cool. 'But, if you insist on knowing, it was an employer in Nottingham who thought that my sexual favours came with the salary. Just as you do. I was very young then, Mr Oliver, and he made my life hell for six months, because I was terrified of losing my first job.'

She saw his face change. Remembering that period of her life was having a salutary effect on the heat in her veins. Suddenly, she felt much more in control of herself, much more like the efficient secretary she usually was than like the melting voluptuary he'd turned her into so easily!

'What happened?' Blaize demanded quietly.

'Eventually I realised that I was my own woman, and that I *did* have a choice. I walked out, and it took me a long, long time to find another job. But it was worth it, in the end. They call it sexual harassment, though I doubt whether you'd have the faintest inkling what it feels like.'

'Oh, hell,' Blaize said in a strained voice, all the tension fading out of him as he released her. 'Leila, I'm so sorry...'

'No,' she said cruelly. 'I doubt whether you're sorry. How many of your employees have you treated in exactly that way? How many pretty little typists have you taken a fancy to, seduced and forgotten in the same day?'

'Leila, you're a long way off beam,' he said urgently, his eyes dark and intense. 'I've never forced my attentions on any woman who didn't welcome them.'

'Can you be so sure?' she challenged. 'You seem to take an especial pleasure in forcing yourself on me, despite all the signals I keep giving you that I don't want to get involved with you!'

'The signals you give out are not nearly as unambiguous as you imagine,' he said forcefully. 'You want me, every bit as much as I want you, and all your protestations to the contrary are just so much flammery.'

'Funny,' Leila replied cuttingly. 'That's just what *he* used to say.'

Blaize stepped forward, and took her hands in his. His voice gentled. 'This man who—who interfered with you...did he hurt you badly?'

'You mean did he get what he wanted?' she replied coldly. 'Is this sympathy, Mr Oliver, or just curiosity?'

'It's an attempt to understand you, Leila.'

'You only understand what you *want* to understand. As for what happened, I leave it to your imagination.'

Blaize's face tightened with anger, as though his imagination wasn't painting very pretty pictures for him.

'If I knew who he was——' He broke off, his mouth a hard line. 'You seem convinced that I spend my life having affairs with women,' he said quietly. 'I don't know how you got that idea, but it just doesn't square with the truth. I suspect it's a fantasy of yours. But I really am not the heartless Don Juan you'd like me to be. I'm not telling you I'm an angel, but——'

'Please.' Leila disengaged her fingers from his. 'You don't have to justify anything you do. It's hardly my business.'

He ignored her interpolation. 'As for my making a habit of seducing my employees, that's nonsense. I never do it.'

'You did it with the last two temps who worked for you,' she cut in coldly. 'Don't they count? Or do you have to be on the permanent payroll to escape the Blaize Oliver seduction routine?'

'Who gave you that little bit of poison?' he asked sharply. 'Ah. Don't bother to tell me. My dear little daughter Tracey.'

'Yes. Your own daughter.' Her nerves were quivering at the confrontation. 'Are you going to tell me that she's a liar, as well as hard and self-sufficient?'

'No, I'm not going to tell you that. But I will tell you that Tracey understands far too little about the world for her intellect.'

'I have the same problem myself,' Leila said ironically. 'I'm tired, Mr Oliver. I'm not paid to be a child-minder, but I don't mind helping out with a sick little boy. When it comes to pandering to the little boy's father, however, my services end!'

His eyes held hers for a few seconds, anger glittering in them. It was as though the shuddering passion they'd shared such a short time before had never happened at all.

He shrugged dismissively. 'Go on, then,' he said drily. 'Take your carefully measured little personality to bed. I'm not stopping you.'

'Thank you,' she told him with elaborate politeness, and went through the silent house, up the stairs to her room. She was shaky and weak. Being with him was more gruelling than running a marathon. One moment they shared the fiery intimacy of lovers, and the next they were snarling at each other like cat and dog...

She had to pass Terry's room on her way. She hesitated, then turned back to open his door silently. By the soft night-light she could see that the boy was sleeping peacefully. The camomile had done him good. She slipped into the darkened room to pull the covers up around his neck, and bent to kiss his forehead lightly.

A tiny noise behind her made her straighten quickly and turn round. There was a shadowy figure curled up in the armchair in a corner of the room. It was Tracey. Leila could see her bare toes poking out from beneath the quilt she'd wrapped round herself. She'd obviously decided to watch over her little brother tonight.

For a moment she thought the girl was asleep, but then she saw the flicker of light on her eyes. Did she know that Leila and her father had been alone downstairs together? Had she heard the quarrel, spied on those flaring moments of passion?

But Tracey made no acknowledgement of her presence, and Leila slipped out, closing the door behind herself. It was nearly one o'clock in the morning.

She showered in her room, washing the stickiness from her skin, then slid between the cool sheets of her bed.

She was thinking with an ache of the effect Blaize had on her.

He was so strong, so damnably attractive, that there was no way she could be indifferent to him. He was able to move her so deeply! He had a kind of pagan magic in him, a magic that made her his slave each time he touched her.

Her stomach was still painful with nerves and emotion. Why was it that every meeting with him left her shaking and disturbed, unable to be at peace with herself for the unhappiness and confusion inside?

Because you're *stupid*, she told herself angrily. You let him get under your skin. You give way to his seduction. You make it easy for him to upset you, by telling him every secret you've got! You give him power over you, and what does he give you in return? Nothing. Just the same ruthless proposition he makes to every pretty woman who takes his fancy. It's just sex. It's just chemistry. You know how potent hormones are, they can make you crazy, or make you feel on top of the world. Every woman knows that.

She opened her eyes in the darkness, and stared at the square of dim light that was her window, deliberately turning her thoughts away from Blaize to that earlier, hateful memory.

It had been years since she'd thought of Mr Martin. Why did Blaize find it so easy to put his finger on all the wounds in her psyche?

He'd been middle-aged and heavily built, the regional manager of a transport firm where she'd got her first job. The office had been arranged so that she and Mr Martin were cut off from the rest of the business, and it had been simplicity itself for a man like that to take advantage of the shy, naïve girl she'd been then.

He'd known that she'd grown up in care, and had no family to back her up.

Her first job. She'd been so frightened of losing it, so frightened of letting down all the people who were looking to her to make a success of her life. She hadn't had the faintest idea how to defend herself from exploitation.

It had started with the odd pinch, with sly allusions that she hadn't understood at first. Then he'd begun boasting to her of his sexual exploits with other women. Telling her blue jokes.

When he'd started realising that she was too nervous of him to complain to his superiors, and too inexperienced to know how to stop him otherwise, the long, nightmare slide had begun. For a long summer and autumn he'd made her life a misery, touching her every time he got the chance, trying to force kisses on her, pressing his body up against her when he passed her desk, which was twenty times a day.

The jokes had got cruder, the approaches more brutal. Her life had reached a low point that she'd never known in all the years of loneliness. She'd fought him, all alone, until he'd made what he really wanted quite plain.

'I'll get you the sack if you don't do it. And I'll make sure you never get another job in this town.'

He'd actually written out her dismissal notice, and had gloatingly shown it to her.

She'd realised then that she faced a crossroads. If she gave in to him, her life would go one way. If she didn't, it would go another. She'd had to make a decision.

She'd known that, if she let him sack her, she'd find it almost impossible to get another job in Nottingham. So she'd walked out of the firm that afternoon, and had never gone back.

'But *why*, Leila?' the social worker had asked angrily. 'Don't you know how hard it is to get a good job like that in these times?'

'I'll get another,' she'd answered flatly.

It had taken months—months in which she'd had time to reflect, to realise that she'd been a fool to give in to Mr Martin's very first smutty joke.

That she must never give in again, not if she wanted to keep her own self-respect.

And after the winter, her next job. She'd come across Mr Martins there, too, but this time they'd been a lot less purposeful, and she'd been a lot less innocent, and she'd known how to stop them, right at the stage of the first blue joke, the first 'accidental' brush against her breasts.

That was one of the reasons she'd eventually gone to Carol Clarewell, once she had the necessary skills and experience—to avoid ever having to face Mr Martin or his like again. And she'd never had that kind of trouble again, not in the three years she'd been with Carol.

In fact, she had stayed so wary of men that she was still a virgin. Blaize had, unwittingly, put his finger on the point.

Oh, there had been men, plenty of them, who had wanted her. But she had never wanted any of them badly enough to go beyond a certain point.

At twenty-four, it had started to worry her. Was Blaize right? Would she end up a cold and hopeless spinster one day?

Her virginity was a precious thing to her, though. Not something she would bestow on any man, just for the sake of losing it. She wanted to give it to a man she loved, someone who would mean everything to her.

Would he understand that? Would he guess that a large part of her coldness and desire to put him off was fear— the fear of a woman who had never known a man's love?

She had been deliberately cruel in comparing Mr Martin to Blaize Oliver. She'd wanted to hurt him, to stop him from doing what he was doing to her.

Yet wasn't Blaize, in his way, just as bad? There was an obvious difference, of course, in that Blaize didn't need to put any pressure on his victims. That awesome sex appeal did the job for him. No doubt he was right, by his lights. Most women were only too eager to fall into bed with him. And no doubt there were very few of them naïve enough to imagine that there was some kind of permanent commitment on his part.

But the principle was the same. He was a man to whom women were a commodity, to be used and exploited as it suited him.

'I don't want a wife, Leila. I don't want one, and I don't need one. I can do without that kind of restriction in my life.'

The memory of his touch passed like fire across her skin.

Why was it, she wondered as she slipped into sleep, that the most beautiful men were always the most ruthless?

The next weekend was feverishly hectic. On Friday night, a party of eight friends of Blaize's arrived from London to stay at the villa. The ensuing party lasted until the early hours. On Saturday morning, six more arrived, making fourteen in all.

And Leila knew that on Saturday night another party was scheduled. 'Nothing elaborate,' Blaize had said airily. 'Sixty or seventy guests, no more.'

The big house seemed to be creaking at the seams. Extra staff had been drafted in from the nearby village to help out, creating even more of a crowd. Leila felt desperately sorry for little Terry. His rash was at last starting to fade, but he was still a sick little boy, and his rest was disturbed by the music, the noise, and the continual procession of friends coming to see how he was.

Luckily, the weather was beautiful, which kept most people out of doors. Blaize had a bar and a stereo system moved out to the pool, so that the racket was more or less inaudible from the house. The guests who weren't

down at the beach, or being flown round the coast by
Rick Watermeyer, or simply sitting talking to Blaize, all
congregated at the beautiful, pillar-lined pool to splash,
sunbathe and party. Sun-umbrellas had been set up. A
barbecue seemed to be on the go all day long, and the
atmosphere was one of continuous carnival.

Most seemed to be young people, in the twenty-to-
thirty age-bracket. Some appeared to have only a passing
acquaintance with Blaize Oliver—he was the sort of man,
she gathered, who was generous with his hospitality and
his invitations—and were simply intent on having fun.
There was no shortage of pretty girls, blissfully trying
out new swimsuits in the Spanish sun, and bright young
men chatting knowledgeably about 'the market', or the
best place to buy a used Porsche.

The older ones, the ones who came to see Terry in his
bed, were obviously much better friends. She heard the
name Vanessa mentioned in conversation, and gathered
that these were people Blaize had known a long time,
since before his divorce.

Leila herself, though, had little chance to assess
Blaize's guests, or mingle with them; Saturday was also
proving to be the day when Blaize's business empire re-
ported in to the big boss.

Not that she was missed in any way. Katherine
Henessey, resplendent in a silk kaftan, was proving a
charming and very competent hostess, marshalling and
co-ordinating the entertainments with an adeptness that
bore out Blaize's tribute to her social skills.

So Leila worked in the attic with the machines most
of the time. Holiday or no holiday, the amount of information that was coming in over the phone, on the
fax machine, or down the telex, was quite bewildering.
Given that Blaize had several departments in London
organising and filtering the data that kept coming in,
there was still too much to handle. Her part of it was

relatively simple. She wasn't expected to know everything that was going on.

But she was realising that it would take months to
train a proper personal assistant—someone who could
decide what was urgent and what was not, what was relevant for Blaize's attention, and what could be shelved.
She herself had little idea.

Reluctant as she was to bother her employer at a time
like this, some of the material that was coming in seemed
to require his urgent attention, and when a Manchester
director phoned in for the third time in two hours,
sounding slightly hysterical, Leila decided that Blaize
would have to be summoned.

He was out at the pool, someone told her. She hurried
across the lawn to locate him among the happy crowd.

'Hel-*lo*.' A good-looking man in his early thirties
blocked her path. 'I don't think we've met.' He smiled,
giving her an appreciative once-over. 'My name's Jason
Tennant. What's yours?'

'I'm not a guest,' she told him, trying to locate
Blaize round his shoulder. 'I'm only Mr Oliver's secretary——'

'The delectable Leila?'

'Well, yes,' she said in surprise. 'I'm Leila Thomas.
How did you know?'

He smiled, showing good white teeth beneath a dashing
moustache. '*Only* is not the word, my dear. Blaize has
been singing your praises to us. Have some champagne.'

'Actually, I'm in rather a hurry——'

But he had already put the cool glass in her hands.
'It's Saturday,' he said firmly. 'And you're much too
pretty to be working indoors on a glorious day like this.
You can take five minutes off to talk to me, surely?'

She smiled, despite herself. 'I must speak to Mr Oliver
right now. It's quite urgent.'

'Does *Mr* Oliver look as though he's in the mood for
urgent business?' Jason Tennant asked meaningfully. She

followed his glance. Blaize, wearing cool, crisp white, was talking lazily to a very nubile brunette in a yellow bikini at the opposite side of the pool. There was rather a lot of the brunette spilling out of the bikini.

'Don't tell me,' Leila said drily. 'His sister?'

Jason grinned. 'I see you've had a few insights into Blaize's character.'

'Hmm.' Katherine Henessey was evidently busy somewhere else right now. If the bikini-clad brunette wasn't careful, she was going to find little Tracey Oliver putting rat poison in her champagne.

Jason Tennant clinked his glass against hers. 'Don't let that go flat. It's Spanish, but it's not bad at all.'

Leila took a sip of the cool champagne. As he'd said, it was delicious. And the tall, smiling man with the moustache had an easy charm that suddenly made the prospect of going back to work less than inviting.

'Are you really the model of efficiency that Blaize makes you out to be?' Jason enquired, looking down at her from his height of over six feet. 'If you won't be offended by my saying so, girls with your sort of looks don't usually bother cultivating anything so practical as an orderly mind.'

'That sounds very much like sexism to me,' she warned him, amused.

'It's fact. Why should they? Men don't want brains in a pretty girl. Most men, that is. I'm a lawyer, and I appreciate intelligence—I see enough stupidity every morning to last me the rest of the day.'

'I can imagine.'

'Are you coming to the party tonight?'

'I'm not sure. It depends on what Mr Oliver wants.' She took a last sip, sighed regretfully, and gave him back the glass. 'That was lovely, but I'm afraid I really do have to do my duty.'

'Blaize won't thank you,' Jason warned, taking the glass. 'But I'll keep this chilled for you. I hope I'll see you tonight.'

She smiled her thanks at him; he was the first person here who'd made any attempt to be really nice to her. Then she walked round the pool, side-stepping basking forms, and approached Blaize and his playmate.

Blaize's expression didn't suggest that he was very pleased to have his conversation interrupted.

'Oh, it's you,' he grunted, looking at her from under dark brows. 'What is it?'

'There are one or two things I think you might want to attend to,' she told him. 'There have been some priority telexes from America and the Far East. And Mr Lewis from Manchester has been on the line three times already, and he says it's most urgent. I can't keep putting him off.'

Blaize gave her a grim look, and rose wearily. 'I'll be back,' he promised the brunette in that special, husky purr that Leila knew so well.

'I'm sure this won't take ten minutes,' Leila said as they walked back to the house. 'I think it's urgent, otherwise I wouldn't have interrupted what was obviously such a fascinating conversation.'

'What are you talking about?' Understanding dawned. 'Ah. You thought I was flirting with Sally.'

'I'm sure that your friend in the yellow bikini will be waiting loyally when you get back.'

'Why the drip of acid? Is this part of your general plan to stabilise my life-style for the benefit of Tracey and Terry?'

'I'm not the interested in your life-style,' she assured him. 'But you *did* employ me to be your secretary.'

'More fool me,' he commented drily. 'You're a prig, a prude and a pain in the——'

He bit back the word. She smiled blandly at him as they entered the house, which was cool after the hot sun. A group of people were talking noisily in the lounge, but they got past without being side-tracked, and turned to go up the stairs.

CHAPTER FIVE

It took him longer than ten minutes to get through the problems posed by the man in Manchester. An hour and a half had gone by before he terminated the last call, and spun on the chair to face her.

'Damn,' he said with feeling. 'And I was so relaxed before you called me.'

'I expect your friend in the yellow bikini is still waiting patiently,' Leila reminded him, and couldn't help adding sweetly, 'She looked like a very relaxing companion.'

'Sally's an old friend. Nothing like that whatsoever.'

'Oh?' Leila said politely.

'Quite frankly, I was dying of tedium out there.'

'That's not very flattering to the poor girl,' Leila said.

'It's not her fault. She's a nice enough person. It's just that...'

'She bores you?'

'Most women do,' he admitted, and rose to stretch taut muscles. The deep green eyes met hers, and Leila could almost feel the tension in them. 'I never seem to find a woman who's both relaxing and interesting.'

'Not even Katherine?'

'Katherine's the exception.' He shrugged. 'As for the rest... Sally in the yellow bikini is relaxing, but about as interesting as watching paint dry.' He gave her a vinegary look. 'Whereas you, for example, are definitely interesting. But about as relaxing as a little blonde viper.'

'Vipers don't have hair,' she said, unable to suppress a snort of laughter at the image.

'You're beautiful when you smile,' he said, watching her thoughtfully. 'Why don't you smile more often, Leila?'

'I smile when I'm happy,' she told him.

'Well, you can't be very happy in my company, because I never see you smile.'

'I'm happy enough when I'm doing my job,' Leila said. 'I only get unhappy when I feel things getting out of control.'

The telephone started ringing insistently, and she reached for it. But he beat her to it, his strong fingers closing around her own. 'I'll take it.'

The conversation was brief, Blaize's gruff irritability clearly overawing the unfortunate person on the other end of the line. He put the receiver down hard, and glanced round the room with anger in his eyes. 'Sometimes,' he said softly, 'I'd like to pull the plugs on all these machines, and just spend one afternoon of my life in peace.'

Leila said nothing. She could understand his desire to be free of all this clutter. But she couldn't see a solution. A man like Blaize couldn't just walk out of his responsibilities. Too much depended on his making the right decisions, twenty-four hours a day. There were people at the other end of those fax and telex machines—people whose own lives and jobs depended on the profits that Blaize had to ensure.

'There's something built into the fabric of big business,' Blaize said wearily, as if reading her thoughts, 'which I call the Doomsday Factor. It's a law that says there's no middle area between expansion and contraction.' He looked down at her with a brooding expression. 'An outfit the size of mine has to keep expanding. I've got to keep acquiring new companies, got to keep finding new areas to deploy the profits that my operations are already generating. Do you understand what I'm saying?'

'Yes,' Leila nodded, 'I understand.'

'At least a quarter of my workload is involved in finding suitable new avenues for investment, available businesses that will fit in with my present holdings, and complement the needs I've got. Ever played gin rummy? You start off with individual cards, and then assemble a sequence, trying to build up a pattern that makes some sense. That's what big business is like. A process of wondering which cards to pick up, and which to put down. Except you never get to the point of throwing down your hand and winning.'

He sounded so taut that Leila knew better than to needle him. 'You're winning all the time, surely?' she said gently. 'You must be making a mountain of money.'

'Money's a dangerous commodity.' He shrugged. 'It burns, Leila. You can't leave the stuff lying around, because it just generates problems. You have to keep it working, or it works against you. And that means *you* have to keep working. Working, and employing others to work for you. Until it becomes a moot point as to whether you control your money, or your money controls you.'

'You seem very much in control to me,' she told him, staring up into the dark, handsome face. 'What's making you so dissatisfied?'

He glanced at her, then laughed. 'Sorry. Have I been doing the poor-little-rich-boy routine? Pay no attention. I'm getting senile, that's all. But thanks for listening.'

'Don't thank me. I'm paid to listen,' she reminded him briskly, and turned to walk back to her desk.

She didn't hear him come up behind her and she started as his strong arms slipped round her waist, drawing her back against his muscular body. 'Oh, yes. I forgot,' he said huskily, his mouth close to her ear. 'Flesh and blood aren't your line, are they? You only listen to me because you're paid to.'

'I didn't say that.' Her hands had closed around his arms to make him release her. But, instead of pulling free, she was snuggling back into his embrace, her own body contradicting her mind with mutinous obstinacy. Why couldn't she resist his touch, damn it? Why was she starting to melt inside at his closeness?

'How about a real challenge, Leila?'

'What is it?'

'For once in your life, just for today and tomorrow, why not try and be interesting *and* relaxing, for my benefit? Just try not to upset me, or fight me, or answer me back, and I'll give you marks out of ten when the weekend's over.'

She arched her neck back, knowing her silky hair would brush his face. 'No, thank you,' she declined.

'Why not?'

'Because your idea of being interesting and relaxing doesn't fit in with mine,' she said pointedly. 'We've already proved that.'

'I'm not talking about sex,' he growled. He turned her round to face him, his smile wicked. 'Though, heaven knows, nothing would do you more good than——' His eyes told her exactly what he thought would do her most good, and Leila flushed.

'Yes, I know exactly what you have in mind,' she said primly. 'But if you're not talking about that, then what are you talking about?'

'I'm talking about coexistence. Can't you bring yourself to be pleasant for once in your life?'

'I'll try,' she said stiffly. '*If* you'll promise not to take advantage.'

'Take advantage?' For a moment she thought he was going to hit back with some retort, but he bit down the comment. 'Very well,' he decided, and let her go.

Leila had to suppress her sigh as he released her. It was almost painful to be released from that possessive, comforting embrace.

'I don't want you stuck in your room tonight,' he added as he turned to go. 'Get something smart on, and circulate.'

'Is that an invitation to your party?'

'You're damned right it is,' he grinned, and left her to her work. She turned to the screen, lost in thought. He really did seem to be on edge; sometimes the most casual things she said angered him, as though she'd got under his skin somehow.

Unlikely, she reflected with a dry smile. It would need a harpoon to get under *that* rhinoceros hide. Business pressures were obviously getting to him. She'd almost have been tempted to call it a mid-life crisis, except that Blaize was not even forty, and as fit and strong a man as she'd ever known.

Her fingers flew across the keyboard, writing up letters while her mind drifted on to other topics, a skill she'd developed long ago. What he'd told her this afternoon was something she'd already learned about big business—the relentless pressure to expand and achieve that sometimes made people crack, or turn to illegal ways of cutting the corners.

That was something a woman like Katherine Henessey, who'd never worked in a business, and whose life had been one of ease and amusement, would never understand. She saw only the power and the glory, but not the way it ate up your time and your life.

But Blaize's annoyance with it all was just a passing thing, surely? Someone with Blaize's resources thrived on challenge and success. Blaize was a typical high achiever. Brilliant at everything he did, physically and mentally head and shoulders above the rest. The classical tycoon.

Or was he? Blaize was superb, yes, but in some subtle way he was different from other top businessmen. Different from the sort of successful people she'd met through her work. More...

More what? More human?

Yes. All too human, she thought wryly. Right now, Blaize would be curling up with Sally in the yellow bikini. Boring or not, she looked as though she had what it took to make an hour or two pass away pleasantly.

Leila swallowed down the acid spasm of jealousy. Why should she be bothered by the way Blaize was with women? If you had the power to keep conquering, then why should you resign yourself to one woman? Sex—like money, of course—was both a slave and a master. It kept some people running for most of their lives, moving from one shallow experience to the next.

She recalled what Blaize had said about how he found it so easy to make money that it was banal to him. Perhaps it was that way with his sexual conquests, too.

Maybe that was the truth of it—that Blaize Oliver, for all his success, simply didn't have enough of a challenge in his life any more. He'd made it to the top in every sense, and now he was wondering where to go next.

Where *did* you go from the top? The only way was down.

Maybe I am better off than you, Mr Blaize Oliver, she thought, turning to the big laser printer to make hard copies of her work. You're a man on a treadmill. But, in a couple of weeks, I'll be able to get off, and you'll be stuck on it.

The evening-dress Leila picked had seen a lot of service over the past year, but she loved it. It was fairly minimal—sleeveless, with a low neckline and a hemline high enough to show her pretty knees—but its thorough-bred lines had come from one of the best young de-signers in London, and it had a charming oversized bow at her waist. And the colour, a shimmering blue, set off her colouring to perfection. She anointed her throat and temples with her current favourite perfume, Poison, and contemplated herself in the mirror.

Not bad. When glossed with a wine-red lipstick, instead of the neutral shades she used through the day, her mouth took on a lush, velvety quality that was distinctly erotic. And when the tan eye-shadow was substituted with the smoky blue that enhanced, rather than toned down, her vivid aquamarine eyes, the total effect was startlingly different.

Well, she shrugged mentally, she was going to be mixing with sixty-odd people tonight, including the flatteringly attentive lawyer, Jason Tennant, and there was no necessity to maintain that low profile she usually took such pains to cultivate. Discretion wasn't necessary at a party!

She looked sexy and desirable. And, wrong as it was, she couldn't wait to see the look in Blaize Oliver's eyes when he saw her. Just thinking about it made her feel momentarily weak.

Before she went down to the party, which was already in full swing, to judge by the dozens of cars parked in the garden and the throbbing music that pulsed up the stairs, she paid a quick visit to Terry in his bedroom. He was sitting up, still flushed, but looking better. Tracey was cross-legged on his bed, playing him at draughts.

'Gosh,' Terry said, wide-eyed as Leila joined them on the bed. 'You look...different!'

'Well, it's the same old me.' She smiled. But he couldn't take his eyes off her: green eyes, so like Blaize's, flattering in their intensity. Like Tracey's, his hair was chestnut and curly, and he had inherited traits from genes very different from Blaize's. Their mother, she guessed, was a petite brunette with curly hair and olive skin. When he grew up, Terry was going to break a lot of hearts, like his father; but that would not be for a long time yet—he was still all little boy. 'Who's winning?' she asked, nodding at the board.

'Me,' Terry said proudly. 'She usually wins, but tonight it's me.'

Tracey said nothing, obviously uncomfortable at having Leila here. Leila laid her cool fingers on the boy's cheeks and forehead.

'You're a little cooler. Feeling any better?'

'I've still got a headache.' He frowned. 'And I get so hot at night...'

'It'll go away,' she soothed. 'You're getting better, I can see that. In a few days you'll be back on the beach, and all this will be just a dream to you.'

'You smell lovely,' he sighed. 'Like flowers.'

She smiled, and glanced at Tracey, who was in jeans and a T-shirt. 'Aren't you coming to the party?' she asked casually.

'I might do.' Tracey shrugged, not lifting her long-lashed eyes. 'Later, maybe.'

'You'll enjoy yourself. There are all sorts of lovely goodies to eat, too. I saw Mrs Saunders putting them out.'

'Yeah,' Tracey said, in a fair imitation of her father's non-committal grunt. 'What's that perfume you're wearing?'

'It's called Poison.' She held out her wrist to Tracey. 'Do you like it?'

Tracey sniffed, and shrugged. 'It's OK. Better than the stuff Dad lets me buy.'

'Borrow some of mine,' Leila said easily, making it an olive-branch. 'The bottle's on my dressing-table.'

She rose with a rustle of silk before the girl could think of a snub, and brushed the boy's fringe away from his forehead. 'Good luck with the rest of the game.'

'Will you come and kiss me goodnight?' the boy asked, looking up at her with those haunting green eyes.

'If you like,' she said, taken aback at the request. 'I don't know what time it'll be...'

'I'm a light sleeper,' he said. The phrase was so obviously borrowed from his father that Leila couldn't repress a smile.

'OK.' She nodded. 'Catch you later. I'm off.'

She was conscious of his eyes following her wistfully as she let herself out. Poor little kid. Neither of them ever talked about their mother, she'd noticed. The topic was a taboo one, either because their father had forbidden it, or because it was too painful to discuss with outsiders. She'd have given a lot, though, to know what brother and sister said to each other in private...

The first person she bumped into downstairs was Katherine Henessey. The kaftan had been replaced by a black evening-dress with more than a hint of Twenties glamour. A very elegant, very formal, very much mistress-of-the-house sort of dress. Katherine gave Leila a slow once-over, as though assessing just how much the blue dress had cost. Reassured that it hadn't cost a tenth of what her own outfit had cost, she smiled without comment on Leila's appearance.

'Snacks in the dining-room, drinks in the lounge, dancing on the terrace,' she said succinctly. 'Eligible men everywhere.'

'Thanks.' Leila smiled. 'Anything I can do to help?'

'I'll let you know if there is,' Katherine informed her with cool eyes. 'Why not have some fun for once?'

'That sounds like a good idea.' Realising that she was ravenous, Leila headed straight for the dining-room, intent on sustenance.

There was a crush round the table, but a kindly middle-aged male got her a heaped plate of crab salad and a glass of wine, and she drifted out to the terrace, where, as Katherine had promised, twenty or more people were dancing to the electronic beat of the latest best-selling album.

There was no sign of Blaize, who was probably holding court in the lounge. But this was where the younger people had congregated. It didn't take more than five minutes for a little group to have formed around her, consisting mainly of appreciative young men, and, before she'd had time to eat as much crab salad as she'd have liked to, she was being whisked across the terracotta tiles by an energetic young stockbroker who'd made it his mission in life to show her the latest disco steps.

As she relaxed, the evening suddenly became fun—more fun than she'd had in months. The stockbroker was displaced by two others in quick succession, though not before he'd had time to yell an invitation to a weekend at Henley over the music. What a joke. When was *she* ever going to get a weekend off at Henley?

The third was the most interesting so far—long-haired and outrageously dressed in a lime velvet suit, he turned out to be the head of an up-and-coming recording company in London. He talked knowledgeably about some of her favourite groups, and appeared to be on intimate terms with some of the most famous names in pop. She didn't believe all his stories, some of which were very wild indeed, but he was different, at least, from the yuppie clones who were still chattering about the markets in stocks and used Porsches.

She spent the next hour dancing and talking with him, until he suggested taking her and a bottle of Blaize's best cognac up to her bedroom, when she decided she didn't want to be *that* different, and disengaged herself as deftly as she could.

Escaping through the crowd, she was confronted by a tall, moustached man holding out a glass of champagne.

'I've been keeping this chilled for you all day,' Jason Tennant said with a smile, 'just as I promised.'

'Now that's what I call service.' She laughed, accepting the drink. 'Thanks, Jason. You've turned up in the nick of time.'

'Was your friend in the velvet suit getting too pressing?' he enquired. The aspiring pop music magnate was retiring from the chase in the direction of the bar;

Jason was almost as tall and broad as Blaize Oliver himself.

'Well...'

'He's notorious,' he told her as she hesitated diplomatically. 'You're much safer with me, I assure you.'

'Thanks.' She smiled, knowing he was being deliberately modest. He was a very handsome man in his quiet, confident way. He had the smooth class that went with a good education and a good job. 'Actually, I didn't want to hear any more about the rock music world. It sounds rather bizarre to me. Do you think it really runs on a river of booze, sex and drugs?'

'Absolutely.' Jason nodded. 'I have a barrister friend who defends a lot of cases for the pop industry, and they're a crazy bunch. They always have been. The guy in the velvet suit is no stranger to the inside of a courtroom, either. Cocaine,' he said succinctly as Leila raised her eyebrows. 'He was lucky to get off. But something tells me you're more into serious music. Am I right?'

'I love all sorts of music,' she told him. 'But if I had to pick ten records for *Desert Island Discs*, they'd all be classical ones.'

'Beethoven symphonies,' he guessed, assessing her with deep brown eyes, 'Mozart piano concertos, at least one Italian opera, and maybe...' He tilted his head consideringly. 'Would you include Bach? Yes. You're cerebral enough to go for Bach. *St Matthew Passion*?'

'Not bad,' she smiled. 'But you've left out Rachmaninov.'

'Rachmaninov,' he repeated. 'Ah. The hidden romantic streak among all the classical tranquillity. A heady cocktail, Leila.' He toasted her with a sparkle. 'How did I do otherwise?'

'Remarkably well,' she admitted, unable to quite conceal her flattery at being paid so much attention. 'You must be a mind-reader. Would your choice be similar?'

'I'd have Shostakovich in place of Rachmaninov,' he told her, 'but otherwise, yes, my choice would be the same as yours.'

'I'm not keen on the moderns,' she said, making a face.

'Nor am I,' he agreed. 'Not on the atonal crew, with their horrible chords and peculiar scales. But Shostakovich is a great melodic composer...I'll play you something some time that I guarantee you'll love,' he promised.

'I'd like that.' Leila nodded.

'Anyhow, what are we doing talking about classical music right now?' He appraised her from head to toe, yet somehow, where the same inspection from Blaize would have raised every hackle in her body, from Jason it was a nice compliment. 'You look stunning,' he said warmly. 'The belle of the ball. Care to dance with me?'

'I'd love to,' she smiled, and let him lead her back on to the terrace.

Jason danced well. She put his age at around thirty-five—young enough to be in her age-group, rather than in Blaize's, but old enough to have an intriguing male authority. He had a deep, soft voice, yet he had no trouble in conducting a conversation with her over the hectic music. He must have developed skills of resonance in the courtroom, she decided.

He was not married, he told her, and was a junior partner in a very successful London legal firm, owned by his father. He had first met Blaize through Blaize's ex-wife Vanessa.

'You've never met her,' he said reflectively, when they'd paused for a break and were sitting close together on the edge of the terrace. 'Don't judge her too harshly from what people say about her. The whole thing was a mistake, really. Blaize is a fundamentally serious person, which Vanessa never was. She never took to marriage, and certainly not to motherhood. She wanted

her independence too much. She always blamed Blaize
for putting an end to her acting career. She used to act
under the name Vanessa Lamb,' he added, and a light
went on in Leila's mind.

'Vanessa Lamb! Is *that* who she was?'

Jason nodded.

'I saw her play Eliza Doolittle in *Pygmalion* a few
years ago,' she remembered. 'She was good. Very pretty,
and very lively.'

'Well, she was a lively actress, rather than a gifted
one,' Jason admitted. 'She thought the theatre was in
her blood, but what she really enjoyed was the excitement. She loved an audience. Also, I've always felt
that Vanessa is the kind of person who doesn't want the
real world to intrude too much into her fantasies. Blaize
used to complain that she was always expecting the scene
to change, as though the world were a stage-set, designed for her entertainment.'

'Yet she must have been a charming person?'

'She certainly charmed Blaize.' Jason nodded wryly.
'He thought the world of her—until he finally found out
what she was like. The break-up wasn't his fault. He'd
have put up with anything from Vanessa, if only she'd
been a good mother to the children. But it was obvious
that her influence on them—when she could be bothered
to exert any influence at all—was prejudicial. The break-
up upset them so much that Tracey ended up going to
a child guidance expert for a spell of therapy.'

'Ouch.' Leila winced. 'Poor child.'

'She was only six or seven at the time. When the divorce was finalised, the judge had no hesitation in giving
Blaize custody, and you know how rare that is. Terry
was only a year old! The judge even left it entirely up
to Blaize's discretion as to when and how often Vanessa
saw the kids.'

'Does he ever try and stop her from seeing them, now?'

'I doubt it. Vanessa was relieved, I think, to get shot of them. That sounds brutal,' he admitted with a shrug, 'but I think that's the truth. Blaize would probably have to force her to come and see them, rather than the other way round.'

Leila digested this sadly. 'She's in Monaco now, isn't she?'

'Yes. After she and Blaize separated, she took up with an elderly playboy, Count von Weckelmann. Minor European aristocracy, but very wealthy. He lets her do as she pleases, and enjoys watching her spend his money, which is exactly the kind of set-up she needed. She's very happy.'

'The children must miss her.'

'Yes,' Jason agreed. 'It's a great pity that Vanessa is the way she is, because they're nice kids.'

'It's shocking,' Leila couldn't stop herself from saying angrily. 'If I had two lovely children like Terry and Tracey, I could never leave them like that, no matter what had happened... She must have no heart!'

'Not much of a heart.' Jason smiled. 'You look quite indignant. Have the kids touched *your* heart?'

She considered telling him about Tracey and the airport, but kept her counsel. It wasn't exactly ethical to be discussing her employer with one of his friends like this. But Jason smiled at her, encouraging her to go on with what she was saying.

'Go on—speak your mind.'

'Well... I can't help feeling sorry for them. They're rather forlorn children. Blaize is so strict with them, too.'

'He is. Still, remember he has to be father and mother to them. And he's very concerned that they shouldn't be spoiled.'

'I know,' Leila sighed. 'But there are more ways than one of spoiling a child.'

'Agreed. But how would you go about raising two children in Blaize's position? Have you any idea of just how many dangers there are for kids in their circumstances?'

'The whole thing is that families shouldn't split up in the first place,' Leila said sadly. 'It isn't fair on the children.'

'It never is. Come on, let's dance.'

The next album on the turntable was a collection of slow jazz tunes, given a sultry blues treatment by a good female vocalist with a husky purr in her voice. Jason moved unselfconsciously to take her in his arms, holding her lightly but firmly against his tall frame. 'Tracey certainly needs a mother,' he went on. 'She's getting a bit of a handful these days.'

'She seems to get on well with Katherine Henessey,' Leila said obliquely, opening a whole new area of conversation.

'Katherine is a mother-figure to them.' She realised that Jason was caressing the naked skin of her shoulders, his fingers light and gentle. 'I think Blaize is thinking of asking her to marry him.'

That old pain pierced Leila's heart. 'Do you?'

'Mmm. She'll make him a good wife, and the kids a loving mother.'

'You like her?'

'Mmm.' Jason didn't seem to want to talk any more after that affirmative, partly because his mouth was now pressed against Leila's temple. His fingers were still wandering across her shoulders, his touch pleasant and warm.

With a little sigh, Leila relaxed in his arms. She could have given him a signal that he was moving a little fast for her—which he was—but she did not. For one thing, her thoughts were very much occupied with Blaize Oliver, and his family problems, and for another, it was very pleasant to be held like this, in strong male arms, while they swayed to the seductive music. It was a long time since someone as personable and charming as Jason

Tennant had paid her any attention, and it would be hypocritical to say she wasn't enjoying it.

The danced without speaking for the next couple of tracks. Her mind had been casting back over the past weeks, from her first, heart-stopping meeting with Blaize by the poolside, right up to their clash of swords this afternoon. There was no doubt that there was some chemical reaction between them. Usually, it manifested itself in sparks of anger; but sometimes, like when he'd kissed her, the reaction was a very different one—something much more interesting than mere antagonism. Something that made her stomach squirm inside her.

In your fantasies, you tended to make people something they were not. You forgot about their defects, and enhanced their good aspects. When she thought about Blaize, she tended to remember the look in his eyes as he'd started seducing her, and tended to forget that he'd been surveying Sally in the yellow bikini with exactly that same look, twenty-four hours later.

One thing you could never ignore about Blaize was his sexuality. The way he made you feel as he held you in his arms, his mouth seeking out the vulnerable erotic areas of your body...

She snuggled a little closer to Jason. He was about Blaize's size and height. He even possessed something of Blaize's grace of movement. If she slid her arms round the broad shoulders, she could almost imagine that it was Blaize holding her like this. A Blaize who was gentle and caring, whose mouth was soft instead of demanding, whose caress was loving instead of provocative.

And it was so convincing a fantasy that she shuddered slightly as the husky voice murmured, close to her ear, 'You're so lovely, Leila. I never dreamed I'd meet someone like you out here, someone so special.'

She closed her eyes, and laughed unsteadily. 'Oh, I'm very ordinary, really.'

'No, you're not. You're something very special.'

She arched slightly as she felt his hands caress the silky skin of her arms. It was a dangerous, foolish game—a game that was cruelly unfair on Jason. But it was too sweet to pull away; she couldn't bring herself to stop it just yet, couldn't bring herself to open her eyes and see that it was Jason's face, and not Blaize's, that looked down at her.

A warm hand touched her chin, raising it. She lifted her face blindly.

'No,' she whispered, 'don't——'

But it was too late to struggle. His mouth closed on hers, his kiss as gentle and firm as everything he did. She surrendered to the moment, her body pressed to his. Oh, Blaize, her mind cried, if only it were you...

But the mouth was too gentle, too undemanding to be Blaize's. There was none of the thrusting fire of Blaize's kisses, none of the excitement that made her pulses race.

The spell broken, she pushed away, panting for breath. 'No, Jason. Please!'

'What is it?' he asked, frowning at her, his face flushed with what he was feeling.

'I—I'm sorry,' she said, confused and bitterly ashamed. 'I've been very stupid. Please, forgive me. I didn't want that to happen.'

'You could have fooled me,' Jason said, reaching for her again. 'Just relax. I'm not going to hurt you.'

'No.' She fended him off. 'Don't think badly of me, but I've made—made a stupid mistake. It's my fault. I'm sorry, Jason. Don't be angry——'

The voice that cut into their exchange was deeper and harsher than Jason's.

'Aah, there you are,' Blaize Oliver said, materialising at her side. He was smiling, but there was a dangerous green glitter deep in his eyes, like fire in an iceberg. His fingers closed round her slender arm with a steely force that made her gasp. 'Sorry, Jason. Will you excuse me if I borrow my secretary for a spell?'

'Well, it isn't exactly an opportune moment, Blaize,' Jason said stiffly.

'Too bad about the moment, I'm afraid,' Blaize told him coolly. 'This can't wait.'

'Now, just hang on a minute,' the other man began angrily. 'I was talking to Leila——'

'Is that what it was?' Blaize said with an unmistakable rasp.

'Would you at least let me finish what I was saying to her?'

'No,' Blaize said flatly. 'Seems to me you've said enough as it is.'

'Damn it, Blaize!' Jason said sharply. 'You don't own every woman in the house!'

'No, but I own this one.' Still holding Leila's arm in cruel fingers, Blaize gave him a smile that was not a smile. There was no doubt in Leila's mind that he was very angry indeed. She could feel it in the hand that gripped her, could almost hear it humming in him like high-tension cables.

'If you weren't my host——' Jason's fingers curled into fists.

'Yes?' Blaize enquired silkily. 'If I weren't your host?'

Big as Jason was, Blaize was bigger. Moreover, Leila realised with a feeling like swallowing an ice-cube, he was equipped with a jagged edge that Jason could never match. And Jason probably had no idea just how angry this man facing him was.

'I'm sorry,' she said to Jason in a strained voice, terrified at the thought of a confrontation in the middle of the dance-floor. 'I—I have to go.'

She pressed against Blaize, forcing him to move away. He led her through the crowd, leaving Jason standing with a frustrated expression among the dancers.

They went down the stairs, into the garden, where the chirp of crickets vied with the sultry music. 'You're hurting my arm!' she protested in anguish.

Blaize did not so much release her as half fling her away from him.

'You little tramp!' he said with cold fury. 'I'm not good enough for you, but that smooth-talking son of a lawyer is?'

'You had no right to cut in like that,' she ground back at him. 'You—you're insufferable!'

'And you're a great little actress,' he rasped. 'All that pious talk about how moral you are, and all the nasty experiences you've had—and then I see you practically making love to a man you've never met before, in the middle of the dance-floor!'

'He kissed me once!' Leila snapped. 'And, if you really must know, I was just stopping him when *you* horned in.'

'Is that why you were wrapping yourself round him like a besotted boa-constrictor?'

'I'm not staying out here to be ranted at, Blaize. You can go to hell.'

'You're not going anywhere,' he said with dangerous smoothness, blocking her path as she tried to get past. 'I asked you to show a little diplomacy this weekend. What the hell is this? Your idea of keeping my blood pressure down?'

'You do *not* own me,' she told him, her voice shaking with anger. 'You invited me to this party, Mr Oliver. In my folly, I assumed I'd be able to enjoy myself for once—which, I might tell you, is a damned rare thing in this house! I didn't count on the Doomsday Factor blowing up around my ears. The megalomania of a man who thinks he owns every woman in sight!'

'And I didn't count on your making an unerring beeline for the richest bachelor in the room,' he retorted with insulting contempt.

'I don't know a thing about Jason's financial circumstances,' she said, her voice rising at the implication.
'He was just being kind and friendly to me. If that's a
crime——'

'When I kiss you,' Blaize cut in harshly, 'you kick and
struggle as though I were some kind of leper. When that
overgrown public schoolboy kisses you, you melt into
his arms like a meringue on a hotplate. What's the
explanation?'

The irony of it was so painful that she almost laughed.
If only he knew that it hadn't been Jason Tennant kissing
her out there, but his own ghost! But wild horses
wouldn't have dragged that truth out of her. 'This is all
a little primitive, isn't it?' she said with deliberate
coldness, rubbing her arm. 'I'm going to have one hell
of a bruise tomorrow, thanks to your delicacy of touch.'

'Will you stop swearing at me?'

'If you'll stop shouting at me.'

'You haven't answered my question!' he snapped, his
temperature obviously rising as hers cooled.

'There *is* no explanation,' she replied, trying to move
round the other side of him. 'Maybe it's just that I prefer
his company to yours!'

'Or that you're as false as water.' He leaned against
the wall of the house, his outstretched arm blocking her
escape. His face was taut with anger. 'Know what I
think?'

'No, and I don't want to know!'

'I think you're about as genuine as a three-pound
note,' he said grimly. 'I think you're out for the main
chance, baby blue eyes, and you don't care what means
you use to get it. Only you've picked the wrong target.
Jason Tennant isn't half the man I am. Shall I prove it?'

'No!'

But he was pulling her towards him with force,
crushing her lips in a kiss that was both a punishment
and a caress. She struggled against him in outrage, but

he was so strong. She gasped as he pressed his lips to the delicate bones of her temples, his mouth almost brutal as it roamed over her throat, his teeth grazing the soft flesh of her neck.

'You little bitch,' he whispered, his voice unsteady with emotion. 'How could you let him kiss you like that? Hell, you drive me crazy!'

Treacherous weakness undermined her resistance. She didn't know whether her own moan was of desire or despair as his hand cupped her breast, then, impatient of the covering of her dress, lifted to slide her shoulder-strap down.

The skin of her breasts was warm and silky in his palm. 'See how you want me?' he said roughly as the fierce pangs of pleasure made her press against him, whimpering. 'You can't help it. You were born to be mine, Leila. I need you, I want you...'

He bent to take her nipple in his mouth, the sharp nip of his teeth a torment that was instantly assuaged by the moist caress of his lips and tongue.

Her emotions exploded in a turmoil, making her arch to him, her arms reaching for him.

'You're hurting me,' she whimpered as he crushed her in his arms.

'And you,' he said huskily, 'do you want to know what you do to me?' He took her hand, drawing it down his body to lay her palm against the hard outline of his desire.

An electric shock seemed to surge from him into her as she touched him, desire igniting like a glass of brandy thrown into a fire.

'You've already forgotten him, haven't you?' he demanded huskily. 'One man is as good as another to you. There's a name for the kind of girl you are. Want to hear it?'

Leila moved first, her hurt and anger lifting her hand in a slap that cracked across his cheek before her mind had even got round to forming the intention.

Before he could recover his balance, she darted past him, pulling her dress straight, and flew up the stairs back on to the terrace. If Blaize got his hands on her before his temper had time to cool——

She almost collided with the tall, elegant figure of Katherine Henessey. She stared at Leila. 'Is Blaize with you?' she asked sharply. 'I saw him walk off the terrace in your company just now.'

'No. I mean, yes.' She was out of breath, and heaven alone knew what she looked like, her emotions torn by desire, pain and anger.

'What *do* you mean?' Katherine demanded icily.

Leila took a quivering breath. 'I mean, yes, I did leave with him, and no, he's not with me now. I left him in the garden.'

'Why are you panting?' The pupils of Katherine's eyes, Leila noticed suddenly, were ringed with an icy green line, arctic centres to the warm hazel corneas. 'What's been going on here?'

Before she could answer, a deep voice came from behind her. 'Nothing's been going on.'

Blaize materialised out of the night behind her. His left cheek, Leila noticed with a mingled thrill of alarm and satisfaction, was reddened. He looked, if anything, even angrier than he'd done before they'd left the dance-floor. His smile was humourless. 'Shall we all get back to the party?'

'Yes, of course,' Katherine said, moving to him. 'That's why I came to find you, darling. I don't want you losing yourself in obscure little corners.'

'Obscure little corners is so right,' he said bleakly. 'I lost my way for a moment.'

Ignoring Leila completely, he took Katherine in his arms and planted a warm, passionate kiss right on her mouth.

Leila felt sick as she saw Katherine's eyes close in a moment of sheer pleasure, the force of Blaize's embrace bending her lithe waist backwards. She had no option but to watch helplessly as Blaize's hand moved hungrily down the other woman's flank, smoothing the shapely figure beneath the black silk, as though she were naked to his touch.

She felt hurt enough to bleed. He was paying her back for that slap, and he'd found a way of wounding her that was far more effective than any sting she'd been able to deliver him.

A fourth figure emerged from the crowd to join the group—Tracey, in a pretty red trouser-suit, with her hair tied up in a loose chignon. She looked very adult—a lot more like the girl who'd met her at the airport than the teenager Leila had left playing draughts on Terry's bed. Her eyes took in the scene, but she said nothing.

'You offered to help an hour or two ago,' Katherine reminded Leila pointedly. Her eyes were bright with triumphant malice. 'I think you're needed in the dining-room now, if you don't mind, my dear.'

'I don't mind at all,' Leila said numbly. All her anger and excitement had collapsed into dull depression.

'Good.' Katherine had linked her arm very possessively through Blaize's. Her even white teeth glinted in another smile. 'If you could just help people to fill their plates, I'd be *so* grateful. Make sure everyone gets a bit of the trifle, OK? And make sure there are no dirty plates left lying around. It makes the place look so untidy. You can just drop them off in the kitchen. Quite sure you don't mind?'

'Quite,' Leila gritted, feeling her skin flush crimson with anger.

'You're a dear. Come on, Blaize. Haven't we had enough pop for a while? Let's put some Strauss on, and show them what waltzing's all about.'

She heard Blaize's husky, intimate laugh as he moved off with Katherine. He still hadn't so much as glanced at Leila again, though he touched Tracey's cheek as he left.

Leila stood perfectly still, counting to twenty. A social worker had once taught her to do that, when her emotions started getting out of control.

Some party. Some *bloody* party.

At the end of the twenty, the anger was fading, but the hurt wasn't.

She met Tracey's eyes. The teenager had probably witnessed that flaming kiss between her father and Katherine. She had certainly witnessed Leila's humiliation at Katherine's hands.

But, for a girl whose wishes were all coming true, she didn't look triumphant. In fact, she looked strangely uncomfortable. And as Leila pushed past her without a word, she caught a distinct whiff of a familiar perfume on Tracey's skin.

Poison.

CHAPTER SIX

LEILA awoke the next morning heavy-eyed and irritable.

She preferred not to think back to the events of last night, but a few salient memories would not be repressed. Like the blazing desire that had grown out of their mutual anger. Like the hefty slap she'd landed on her employer's cheek.

Like the next three hours spent dully dishing out food and ferrying dirty plates to the kitchen from the dining-room.

And the amusing spectacle of Blaize all over Katherine for the rest of the evening. Not to mention Jason Tennant dancing very pointedly with someone else, a very pretty girl who'd caught her eye earlier in the evening.

And, at one o'clock in the morning, just when the party was reaching its height, the way Katherine had sent her to bed with effusive thanks for being 'such a helpful pet'.

The only bright point had come in Terry's bedroom. Despite everything, she hadn't forgotten her promise to him, and the way he had snuggled into her arms when she kissed him goodnight had gone some way towards assuaging the indignities and affronts of the evening.

She washed, listening to the silence of the house. Everyone would no doubt be sleeping very late this morning. Blaize, to her certain knowledge, had drunk half a bottle of Glen Grant last night. As if *he* was the one who'd been wounded!

Sunday. Her day off. She would have liked nothing better than to get a hundred miles away from this house and its occupants today. But she didn't have any kind of transport.

At least the pool would be free at this time of the morning. Maybe a good long swim would help chase away the headache and the depression.

She put on her costume, pulled a robe over herself, and went out.

It was a slightly muggy, sultry day. The sky was hazy, rather than overcast, and there was hardly a breath of wind. Not a soul appeared to be stirring, though the sprinkler system was already working, showering its diamonds over the lush lawns.

Someone had made strenuous efforts to tidy up at some stage last night; empty bottles had been gathered in huge wicker baskets, and litter had been collected in black plastic bags. The amount of food and drink consumed was astronomical. This little thrash must have cost Blaize a fortune. She kicked a very expensive-looking pair of scarlet panties aside with distaste. Some party.

The water was cool and delicious. Clearing her mind of everything, she swam a few lengths, and started feeling better. She'd been a good swimmer at school, and had held the record for underwater swimming. Hanging on to the edge, she eyed the distance across the pool. It was a big pool, and a long way. Once she could have made it underwater, at a stretch. But now, after six or seven years of a sedentary existence behind desks?

She decided to try, and took several deep breaths before sinking under the blue water, and kicking out hard for the opposite side.

Her lungs started to burst two-thirds of the way there, and she had a moment of despair. Then the memory of last night's indignities flashed into her mind, and anger fuelled her veins with the necessary energy.

She felt a moment of joy as her fingertips touched the other side, and she exploded out of the water, whooping for breath.

'I was just wondering whether to jump in and pull you out.'

She looked up, spluttering and gasping, to see Blaize sitting on the diving-board, watching her. He was wearing cream denims and a dark blue shirt, and he looked wearily ironic.

'It's been—a long time—since I did that,' she panted, clinging to the edge. 'You're up—early. I expected you to be—dead to the world.'

'I couldn't sleep.'

'Guilty conscience?' she suggested innocently.

'No,' he growled. 'Little men with little pneumatic hammers, working away inside my skull.'

'You drank far too much whisky. I saw you.'

'Sharp-eyed little minx.'

'The water's lovely. I felt the way you look before I jumped in.'

'No, thanks. I took a long time to work up this hangover, and I'm going to enjoy it. Besides, in my present state, I'd probably drown. And I don't trust you to pull me out.'

'After last night's behaviour? You'd be lucky if I threw you a water-wing.' He evidently wasn't going to offer any kind of apology. Well, she'd been silly to expect one. 'What time did you all get to bed?' Leila asked, drifting away and treading water.

'I can't speak for the rest of them,' he said, 'but I crawled off around five this morning.'

Probably into Katherine's arms, she added mentally, and winced unhappily at the thought.

'Go on,' he commanded, 'swim, swim. I'll be all right, as long as you don't splash too loudly.'

Leila swam another couple of lengths before pulling herself out and drying herself on her towel. Blaize's tiger's eyes couldn't resist assessing her slender, athletic body with a rather wry air. She pulled on her robe, and sat down next to him on the diving-board.

'I know a sovereign remedy for hangovers,' she suggested.

'Does it work for viper bites?' he enquired drily.

'You can't blame me for your excesses, either alcoholic or any other kind,' Leila reproved. 'You behaved like some awful old sea-lion last night.'

He arched one dark eyebrow. 'Awful old what?'

'Haven't you ever seen those animals on nature programmes? The males are awesome great beasts, with huge teeth and bad tempers. They collect harems of females around themselves——'

'I get the picture,' Blaize interrupted. 'But I was just defending your honour against that smooth-talking young whelp, Jason.'

'My honour wasn't in any danger,' she said primly. 'And Jason hit the nail on the head when he said that you think you own every woman in sight.'

'Haven't we got this the wrong way round?' he rasped, baleful green eyes piercing hers. 'Shouldn't I be the one getting all moral, and shouldn't you be the one making the apology?'

'Certainly not,' she retorted, and towelled her hair briskly. 'You should be ashamed of yourself.'

'I know what I should do,' he rumbled, 'but I don't think I'm strong enough yet.'

She brushed her damp hair into some kind of order while he watched.

'You should let your hair grow,' he decided, inconsequentially. 'It's too pretty to keep so short.'

'I've just cut it all off,' she informed him.

'Trust you to do something as daft. Your judgement is seriously impaired, Miss Thomas. Sure you weren't dropped as a baby?'

'Only as far as the orphanage.'

The wry remark made them both smile briefly. 'Well,'
Blaize said, rising, 'I have a flying lesson lined up this
morning, after which I have to ferry some of my eager
friends up to France, for a gourmet meal. The duties of
being a host seem to get heavier every year.'

'My heart bleeds.'

He stared into her eyes between narrowed lashes.
'You're not going to apologise, and I'm not going to
apologise, so I guess we'll have to settle for this.'

She had opened her unsuspecting mouth to say something when Blaize took her cool face in his hands, and
kissed her parted lips.

His kiss was hard, warm, and intimately possessive.
It stilled her for a moment, the way a bird can be hypnotised in a man's palm. She felt his tongue touch hers
with wicked intent, just enough to set her hair-trigger
pulses racing. Then he released her, and looked into her
face as if to check that her skin was flushing, and that
her eyes were dazed.

'Try and be good while I'm gone,' he suggested
huskily, and walked away.

Damn him! She tried to recover her composure,
listening to the pounding of her own heart. He knew
how to disturb her all too well...

Once her hair was sun-dry, she picked up her towel
and went back to the house to see if there was any
prospect of breakfast. There was, but the only person
present, sitting with a cup of coffee and a piece of toast,
was Jason Tennant.

Feeling more than a little embarrassed, she bade him
good morning, and joined him.

'Is this safe?' he enquired drily. 'Or will Blaize come
charging in here and brain me with the jam-jar?'

'Oh, he's off for a flying lesson.' She took a welcome
sip of coffee. 'I'm terribly sorry about last night, Jason.
It was all my fault.'

'Well, some of it was evidently mine.' He glanced at her. 'You did give me the impression that my attentions were not unwelcome, you know.'

'I know,' she said, looking wretchedly at her toast. 'I was very wrong.'

'What was it all about? Do you mind telling me?'

'There's nothing to tell. I enjoyed your company, Jason. I really did. You were very kind and attentive. But I didn't want...what happened...to happen.'

'You must have had other things on your mind,' he said drily, obviously half guessing at the truth. 'So what's with Blaize? I thought he was going to hit me, right there in the middle of everybody. When he was telling us all how efficient and charming you were, I didn't suspect that his feelings were quite so strong. Has he appointed himself sole guardian of your honour?'

'Of course not.' She smiled. 'I'm only here for a few more weeks, after which I'll probably never see Blaize Oliver again. His temper is just something I have to put up with until then.'

'He certainly seems to be very touchy where you're concerned. And I get the impression that dear Kate is none too pleased with his interest in you.'

'Oh, you noticed?'

Jason grinned at her tone, then looked at her sideways. 'You're sure you didn't enjoy what happened...last night?'

'I was very flattered, Jason. But I mean it. It's got nothing to do with Blaize, I promise. I'm just not into serious relationships at this stage of my life. But I'd like to be your friend, if you'll let me.'

Jason grunted, and pulled out a pack of cigarettes. He lit one, and blew a cloud of smoke into the air. He was silent for a while. She didn't need to say anything more. Unlike Blaize, with his sea-lion manners, Jason was a gentleman. He'd respect her wishes without challenge. He glanced at the big window. 'Looks like thunder,' he commented. 'Just my luck. A three-day break in Spain, and it rains on my parade. In more senses than one.'

Leila smiled. 'The girl you ended up with last night was much prettier than me.'

'It was like going from French champagne to cheap white wine.' He shrugged. 'What are your plans for the rest of today?'

'To keep out of everyone's way. If I had a car, I'd wander around and see something of the countryside. But I haven't, so I suppose I'll find a shady spot in the garden and read.'

He held something up with a jingle. 'Blaize has given me his Golf to use while I'm here,' he told her, dangling the keys. '*And* there's a map in the glove compartment. What do you say to a tour of the locality, followed by a lunch in some local restaurant?'

'That sounds super,' Leila said fervently. 'But isn't it a bit like playing hookey?'

'No one's going to miss us,' he pointed out. 'Blaize is out, and the rest are all asleep, except Lucy. We can leave a message with her.'

The temptation to give Blaize a thoroughgoing snub was irresistible. He needed a punishment after his insufferable arrogance of last night, and going out with Jason would be just the way of asserting her independence.

'Then I'd love to go,' she agreed decisively. 'Just give me twenty minutes to dress?'

'Go on. I'll meet you at the car.'

Feeling positively light-hearted, she went upstairs to change. The prospect of hitting back at Blaize for once was one she relished, not to mention getting away from Katherine Henessey's little jobs, which, she suspected, would be increasingly numerous from now on.

She slipped into a stretchy towelling dress in a pastel pink. It was slinkily snug over her breasts and hips, but it was very comfortable, and it made her feel as though she were really on holiday. Picking up her camera, a scarf and her dark glasses, she went out to meet Jason.

Tracey's door opened as she passed by, and Tracey's head emerged. 'Hello,' she said.

Leila paused. 'Hi. How's Terry?'

'Sleeping. But he's OK.'

'Did you enjoy the party last night?'

'It was OK,' Tracey said, which was her usual response, whether something had been dull as ditchwater or one long scream of excitement. 'Are you going somewhere?'

'Jason Tennant has asked me to go for a little drive round the locality. Maybe you can suggest somewhere interesting?'

'There are lots of places.' Tracey nodded. 'There's Peratallada, which is an interesting old town. And Pals is very pretty. And Begur is lovely, too. And all the beaches, of course...'

'Sounds good. Got anything planned for this morning?' Leila asked, catching a wistful note in the girl's voice.

'No. And everyone's bound to be asleep until noon.'

'Feel like coming with us?'

Tracey's green eyes lit up. 'Do you mean it?'

'Of course. I can't see you behind that door—are you dressed?'

Tracey opened the door to show that she was in a pair of cream cotton overalls. 'Is this all right?'

'You look lovely.' Leila smiled. 'You can be our official party guide.'

'Great!'

'I'll tell Lucy you're going, then.'

'Great' was at least an improvement on 'OK', Leila reflected as she went downstairs, after having had a word with Lucy, who seemed quite relieved to have Tracey off her hands for the morning. Over the past couple of days,

Tracey had warmed towards her, which puzzled her. She didn't bother questioning it overmuch, however; it would certainly make her life here a little easier not to have *everyone's* hands against her.

Jason wasn't exactly overjoyed to hear that they were going to have company on their trip. He'd obviously been looking forward to having Leila all to himself. But he put a brave face on it.

Tracey arrived five minutes later, complete with guidebook to the area.

It was rather odd being in the all-white VW Golf with Tracey again. It brought back memories. She caught Tracey's eye for a moment, and they smiled at one another with the instinctive warmth of people who shared an amusing recollection. She had learned a lot more, Leila reflected, about this odd, pretty little girl since that strange first day in Barcelona. They set off down the tarmac drive.

The thunder broke at two o'clock in the afternoon, far too late to spoil what had proved to be a delightful morning. By that time, the three of them were just settling down to lunch in a tiny, crowded restaurant in an old hillside town. The first peal rumbled overhead like a steamroller in the sky, and a scattering of fat, wet drops sprinkled the window-pane.

'Just in time,' Tracey commented.

'What are we having?' Jason asked, studying the menu. 'It all sounds intriguing. What on earth is "black rice"?'

'It's cuttlefish cooked in its own ink, with rice,' Tracey explained. 'It isn't very interesting. But *rape* is delicious—it tastes just like lobster.' Leila watched her as she studied the menu over Jason's shoulder. Tracey had proved to be a sweet companion this morning, knowledgeable about the area, but not unmannerly, the way some teenagers might have been. The three of them had enjoyed the tour immensely; it was the closest thing to a family outing, Leila suspected, that Tracey had had for a long time.

Her response to the happy, relaxed atmosphere had been to show unexpected flashes of affection towards Leila. Leila had been careful not to over-respond, but it was nice to feel Tracey showing warmth, rather than cold hostility. For once, it seemed, Tracey had stopped thinking of Leila as a rival for her beloved Katherine.

While they waited for their food to arrive, Tracey gloated over the corals and shells she'd bought in one of the towns on their route. She collected marine things, Leila had learned, and not just for their beauty. She'd revealed an ease with the jaw-breaking names that had surprised Leila. Beneath her interest lay a lively curiosity about the lives and habits of the things she collected. Leila had been so impressed that she'd bought a big, glossy cowrie to add to the haul, much to Tracey's delight.

'I'd love to do marine biology at university,' she said now, in answer to a question from Leila, and pulled a face. 'But I don't think I'm going to get good enough marks. Not if things go on the way they're going.'

'Don't you do well at school?' Leila asked.

'I'm awful,' she confessed with a sigh.

'Well, you've got the intelligence,' Jason said. 'So what's the problem?'

'Oh...the teachers don't like me. Most of them don't, anyway. I suppose I'm rather naughty. Dad's furious with me, because I used to be top of my class. That's why he makes me study, even on holiday.'

Leila caught Jason's eye, and looked away. She could guess the problem well enough. Ever since the divorce, Tracey would have been distracted and rebellious, probably unable to concentrate. The arrival of puberty had, as so often happens, been disastrous; the problem had worsened. When impatient teachers tried to discipline her, she'd have interpreted their reaction as dislike. And the school complaining to Blaize would have added to the pressure at home. The cycle of underachievement and poor behaviour would have built up quickly, and it was a hard cycle to break. Leila knew that. It had happened with her own schooling once or twice during her teens.

Was it worth having a talk to the girl about it? Leila herself wasn't exactly an academic type, but her own experience had given her some idea of what Tracey was going through. She decided to make some gentle approaches to the girl later on, and, if she wasn't snubbed, perhaps see if she could help in some way.

They ate a tasty lunch, accompanied by a full-bodied Rioja, and, after an hour or so, scuttled out through the by now pouring rain to head back to Cap Sa Sal.

'They'll all be sitting around complaining about the weather,' Jason predicted, which turned out to be fairly accurate. Most of the house-guests, plus a few who seemed to have been left over after the party, were sitting in the lounge chatting, and making locustlike ravages into a buffet lunch that was being eaten late, Spanish-style.

Blaize wasn't around, but a very frosty Katherine was on hand to greet them.

She followed Leila out of the lounge, and turned angrily on her. 'What is the meaning of this behaviour?' she snapped.

'I'm sorry? What behaviour?'

'Simply absconding with the child, without even asking for our permission.' Katherine's lips were thin with tension. 'Do you realise that I almost called the police?'

Leila stood very still. 'I really don't see what the police have to do with it,' she said quietly. 'I told Lucy where we were going, and she had no objections.'

'The governess has no authority in this house! She was very wrong to allow an unknown like you to take her employer's child away!'

'In the company of Jason Tennant, who is an old friend of the family,' Leila pointed out. 'I wouldn't have dreamed of taking her out on my own. But Tracey seemed bored, and was keen to come, so I saw no harm in it.'

'No harm? Let me be the judge of what is harmful and what isn't, please. The girl is seriously unstable!'

Leila met the angry, cold eyes. 'Tracey took no harm this morning, Katherine,' she repeated. 'She was at a loose end. And, in fact, she seemed to enjoy herself rather more than she usually does in this household.'

'Just who the hell are you to criticise the way the household is run?' Katherine's eyebrows had soared in outrage. 'As it happens, I had plans to amuse the girl myself this morning.'

'Oh, dear.' Leila tried to make it sound sincere. 'But perhaps you should have told her in advance. I don't see why you're so angry about this.'

'You mean I should be pleased with your incredible behaviour?'

'I mean that Tracey had a happy, carefree morning, which would otherwise have been spent moping around the house. Is—is Mr Oliver upset?'

'Tracey's father is furious,' Katherine said grimly. 'Rick Watermeyer has had to fly him to Gerona in the helicopter, for an urgent meeting, as it so happens. But he'll speak to you himself when he gets back, and I can assure you that you won't find it so easy to be insolent to *him*.'

Leila's heart sank like a stone. 'Very well,' she said heavily, and turned to go.

'You're doing your best to get your hooks into the girl, aren't you?'

Leila stopped and turned round, her face set. 'That's an extraordinary thing to say. What do you mean?'

'Sweet little innocent.' Katherine's tone made the words three icicles. 'You have no intention of helping out with the guests, I note.'

'I didn't know you needed help,' Leila said, blinking at the change of attack. 'There seems to be an adequate amount of staff here.'

'Adequate?' Katherine repeated coldly. 'Two stupid housemaids, and old Mrs Saunders? With everybody congregating indoors because of the weather? Quite apart from anything else, you should have stayed to help out, instead of absenting yourself with Jason Tennant and the child. You do precious little as it is!'

'But I'm not a housemaid,' Leila reminded her calmly. 'I'm Mr Oliver's secretary. My duties don't include helping out in the house.'

'You are Mr Oliver's *employee*,' Katherine said, putting a frigid emphasis on the word. 'And your duties are whatever Mr Oliver decides they are.'

'That's questionable,' Leila replied, trying to control her anger at the way Katherine talked to her. 'But, in any case, I take my orders from him, Katherine, not from you.'

'Well, in his absence, I am in charge in this house,' Katherine replied, in a voice that sounded like skates hissing over ice. 'And I am now asking you to go back into that lounge, and help gather up the used plates and glasses.' She gave Leila's clingy pink dress a grim look. 'But you'd better change out of *that* first.'

Leila met the ice-centred hazel eyes. It wouldn't have cost her much to help out. But she knew very well that things were under control, and that Katherine's imperious commands were intended to humble her, and to make sure she knew her place, and that was something that raised her hackles to the no-return point.

'I'm sorry you have a lot of guests on your hands this weekend,' she said in a voice that was silkily controlled. 'But then, as you've just said, you *are* the mistress of the house. I'm only a hard-working temporary secretary. And this is Sunday, my one day off.'

'You refuse?' Katherine said dangerously.

'I very much doubt that Mr Oliver would expect me to wait on his guests,' Leila replied flatly. 'But, if he does, then he can tell me so himself.'

There were white marks around Katherine's nostrils, as though some invisible devil were pinching her there. Leila turned and walked away, tingling to her toes.

That hadn't been very clever, she realised in retrospect. Katherine Henessey wasn't the sort of enemy she needed. But there had been no way of avoiding a confrontation—not with Katherine pushing so hard. There was going to be an unhappy outcome from that little tussle, of that she was glumly certain. Katherine would make sure of that, if Blaize was every bit as furious as she'd claimed. There would be a full report as soon as he got back from his flight.

Not that much could be done to worsen relations between herself and Blaize, she thought unhappily. In fact, it would not surprise her to find herself on her way back to London early next week.

Well, maybe that would be all for the best. Carol would not be very pleased; she thought highly of Blaize Oliver, and he was a good customer. But Leila had enough faith in her intelligence to know that Carol would accept her explanation of how and why things had gone wrong.

But she was not looking forward to her imminent interview with Blaize.

The rest of the afternoon continued dark and wet. She spent it well away from Katherine and the guests, in Terry's room. They played games with the boy until he drifted off to sleep, and then Tracey took Leila to see her shell collection. It was immaculately kept, and every piece was catalogued with a skill that was quite striking— not at all what would be expected from a girl who didn't do well at school.

A few casual questions about her schoolwork showed that Tracey was in a mood to open her heart to Leila. No doubt Katherine would have classed it as 'getting her hooks in', but Leila was genuinely concerned, and she listened sympathetically to what Tracey had to say. It was an escape from her own problems, at least, to have this glimpse into the troubled world of Tracey Oliver. And if she was to be sent off back to London next week, this was her last chance to do anything for Tracey.

The situation was much as she'd suspected it to be. Tracey was not short of intelligence, or even application, but her concentration had been badly affected since her parents had split up, and relations with her teachers were at an all-time low.

Her father had been sympathetic at first, Leila gathered, but had become increasingly impatient over the past couple of years.

'He's on their side,' was the way Tracey put it. 'There's only Kate who sticks up for me. If Dad married her, everything would be so much better...'

Leila listened in silence. Tracey's faith in Katherine Henessey, she was certain, was misplaced. She'd had time to assess the impeccable Kate, and had found a coldness beneath the charming surface that had disturbed her. Whatever her attractions for Blaize, Katherine was far too selfish and spiteful a person to make a really loving mother to this difficult girl, who'd already once had to have professional guidance. Leila knew in her heart that Kate had been using Tracey, and that, once she was Blaize's wife, her interest in his 'unstable' daughter would rapidly fade.

But that was another issue. The things she wanted to say to Tracey right now were about school, and, in order to get her confidence, she would have to tell Tracey a fair bit about herself, to show her that she really did understand.

'Want to know something about me?' she began, sitting down beside Tracey on the girl's bed.

Tracey nodded.

'I had problems a bit like yours when I was at school.'

'Why was that?'

'Well, it's a long story...'

She missed supper, not really wanting to face Katherine again. Some of the guests were already leaving, their weekend over.

Blaize had not yet returned. She questioned Lucy about his manner.

'Was he angry about our taking Tracey out?'

'He always looks angry to me these days.' Lucy shrugged. 'I'm getting terrified of him. Katherine was angry, that's for sure. She gave me a right blast this morning. For all she's so sweet and ladylike, she can use some awful language sometimes.'

'Did she swear at you?'

'I don't mean swearing. She says things that cut into you, things that really hurt. She really knows how to manipulate people.' Lucy made a face. 'It won't be a happy day for the staff when Mr Oliver marries her. What have you and Tracey been talking about so busily all afternoon?'

'Oh, this and that...'

She went back to her room, and read for an hour or two. Then, as ten o'clock approached, she got up and ran herself a bath. She hadn't showered after her swim that morning, and the smell of chlorine was still on her skin. She was thinking about Blaize and Katherine. Men were such bad judges of women. She'd always felt that. For all his formidable intelligence, Blaize hadn't really known what his first wife, Vanessa, was like. And she suspected that he didn't really know what Katherine was like, either. In common with most men, he often didn't bother to look beyond the surface of a woman, and Katherine took care to show him a highly polished surface.

Ah, well. Maybe women weren't such good judges of men, when it came to that...

She added jasmine bath-salts, so that the water creamed and frothed in fragrant white mounds, and she slipped into the warm water. The sweet smell was infinitely soothing, and she lay back, resting her head. It was good to clear her mind of everything, and just dream.

She was half-asleep when she heard the peremptory knocking at her bedroom door.

'Damn,' she muttered to herself, and rose out of the water, dripping. 'Hang on!' she called aloud as the knocking started again. 'I'm just in the b——'

But the knocker wasn't waiting any longer, and she heard her bedroom door open and close again with a bang. Footsteps headed heavily her way.

With a little gasp, she sank down among the suds again, scooping some of the froth around herself as a frail covering for her nakedness.

The bathroom door opened, and Blaize was framed in the doorway. His tan leather jacket was spattered with rain, and his dark hair was damp. The stare of those tiger's eyes was awesome. Had she been at her most collected, instead of sitting naked and dreamy in the bath, his presence would have shattered her composure. As it was, she quailed behind her flimsy covering of bathfoam, sinking as deep into the water as she could, and drawing her knees up. Her nakedness was covered, but only just.

'Can't I even turn my back for a day?' he rasped, towering over her. 'What the hell have you been getting up to, Thomas?'

'Nothing,' she gasped, wide-eyed. 'You shouldn't be in here——'

'Nothing? The whole bloody household is in a turmoil because of you.' He was too angry to have even noticed that she was stark naked beneath the foam. 'You've been appallingly rude to Katherine, and my daughter's crying her eyes out in her bedroom. For heaven's sake, don't you know that Terry's still sick? Don't you realise that the house is full of guests? Have you no consideration for anybody or anything?'

'B-but what have I *done*?' Leila stammered, going into shock. She'd anticipated hard words, but not this fury.

'I don't know where to start,' Blaize said forbiddingly. 'But let's start with your little jaunt this morning.' He pointed a finger at her like a revolver. 'I told you to stay away from Jason Tennant. You were disobeying my explicit instructions when you went off with him, but you could at least have kept your little dalliances private!'

'Dalliances?'

'You had no damned right to involve Tracey in your misconduct,' he seethed. 'Doesn't it occur to you how vulnerable she is? Did you think you were being clever, using her as cover for your escapade with Jason?'

She felt herself go pale. 'That's a disgusting assumption! It was a harmless outing——'

'And then you had the towering insolence to come back and be abominably rude to Katherine, simply because she asked you for an explanation.' His eyes were smoky with anger. 'Frankly, I can hardly believe some of the things you said to her.'

Frankly, Leila thought wryly, neither could she. No doubt Katherine had given him her own version of the conversation, suitably edited and embellished. 'I can't talk to you sitting in my bath,' she said, trying to haul her tattered dignity around herself. 'Will you just have the decency to let me get dressed——'

'But your prize piece of impertinence was prying into Tracey's private life,' he rasped on, ignoring her interruption. 'What the hell makes you think you've got the right to play amateur psychologist with my daughter?'

'All I did was offer her some advice about her schoolwork! I said nothing that could have upset her! When I left her, she was happy and optimistic.'

'Optimistic?' he sneered. 'You tried to draw some kind of parallel between what Tracey's going through and your own childhood,' he said savagely. 'You had the tactlessness and presumption to do that!'

Leila looked at him in horror. Her little mountain of foam was slowly starting to disintegrate. She hugged her slippery knees. 'I thought it might help Tracey——'

'Help her?' His voice was harsh. 'You and I might have come out of the gutter, but Tracey didn't—thank heaven. There is no connection between the kind of childhoods we had, and the situation Tracey is in.'

Bitterly hurt by his tone, she answered him in a low voice. 'I repeat, all I did was try and give her a little advice about the problems she's having with her schoolwork. I told her something about my own teenage years, because I thought it might be relevant.'

'Well,' he said with sulphuric force, 'all you succeeded in doing was upsetting her to the point where Katherine found her crying hysterically on her bed.'

'She wasn't crying when I left her——'

'I've just seen her,' he grated. 'She's crying now.'

'I—I don't know what can have happened!'

'Don't you?' He put one fist on his hip. 'Well, clever Miss Thomas, if you've got such an insight into my daughter's heart and soul, let's hear what you have to tell me.'

Leila flushed with discomfort. 'You won't like what I have to say.'

'That's par for the course.' He nodded bleakly. 'Go on, anyhow.'

'Well, there is one thing that I know really upsets Tracey.'

'Yes?'

She didn't know how to phrase the damnably awkward thing she wanted to say. 'I—I can understand that you're wary of another marriage. But casual relationships aren't the best thing for children, either.'

He looked into her eyes, making her quail behind her foam barrier. 'I don't understand you.'

'If—if you really want to spare the children pain, then perhaps you should make sure they don't know about your—your——'

His expression was growing even more dangerous. 'My what?' he rasped.

'Your conquests,' she finished on a gulp. 'The girls on the side.'

He stared at her balefully. 'I expected something sensible, not that old chestnut,' he growled.

'Well, you did ask me for my advice——'

'There are no girls on the side,' he said impatiently. 'I won't say that I'm some kind of monk, but I know how to control myself in front of my children. They've never seen me with any loose women, if that's what you're getting at.'

'I don't think you're aware just how much they do see,' she said in a low voice. 'Especially Tracey. She's nearly a woman now, and she understands a lot more than you give her credit for.'

'It wouldn't matter if she were a teenage Einstein,' he retorted. 'There *is* nothing for her to see or understand. Do you think I parade half-naked floozies through the house every night?'

'No. But I do think that you have too many affairs, and that you could be more discreet. I knew you'd be angry,' she concluded unhappily as his face darkened.

'Discreet? Did *Tracey* tell you that I have all these affairs?'

To add to the horrible situation, her stock of foam was dwindling rapidly, leaving her naked to his angry eyes. Leila hesitated, then nodded miserably. 'Yes, Blaize. She did.'

'You're lying,' he snarled.

'Please get out of here,' she said in an anguished voice. 'I've told you what you wanted, and you have no right to interrogate me in my bath like this!'

'Do you think I've never seen a naked woman before?' he said contemptuously. Unexpectedly, he reached out. Iron hands clamped around her arms, hauling her upright.

Leila gasped in pain and dismay, but his strength was overwhelming. His eyes devoured her streaming body, his normally passionate mouth a hard line in his tanned face.

'Let me go,' she said, close to tears of anger and humiliation. *'Let me go!'*

'I ought to——' He bit back the rest of it, his eyes lifting to impale hers. 'The only reason I'm not going to pack you off back to London is because I don't want to embarrass Carol Clarewell. She and I go back a long way, and I'd rather she didn't know just how badly her prize employee has behaved. She thinks more highly of you than you can imagine, though goodness knows why.'

'Have you finished?' Leila asked tightly, her eyes blurred with tears.

'Almost,' he grated. 'Stay away from my children from now on, Leila. And stay away from Katherine. You've done enough damage. I don't want to have to tell you again.'

He released her at last, his fingers leaving livid marks in her creamy skin. Something seemed to explode inside her. Unable to stop herself, she lashed out at him with a sob. Exactly as had happened last night, her slap caught him off guard, landing squarely across his mouth.

'You bully,' she panted, swinging at him again. 'You cruel, arrogant, selfish *pig*——'

He caught her wrists, pulling them down, or else she would have hit him again, even harder. 'Control yourself,' he rasped, immobilising her.

'What for?' she demanded furiously. 'We come from the gutter, don't we? You've got the manners of a gutter hoodlum, so why should I restrain my squalid instincts?'

'Stop struggling, damn you!'

'If I were a man,' she spat at him, 'I'd thrash you! If I only had a brother or a father to defend me—get your hands off me!'

'Not until you settle down,' he said meaningfully.

'I could tell you one or two things about your precious family arrangements,' she said bitterly, pulling away from him as his fingers eased. She snatched up her towel and covered her nakedness. 'Your kids haven't had a kind smile or an understanding word out of you for years. What are you punishing them for? For being half Vanessa?'

'You're being absurd,' he ground out, touching his tender lip, where she'd caught him fair and square.

'What kind of life do they have?' she demanded shakily. She wound the towel around herself, like a sarong. 'You treat them like little adults, expecting them to understand everything, get everything right, and do everything they're told. But you don't give them a scrap of help. They're *not* adults. They're vulnerable, confused children, and they've been hurt more than you can imagine. Children need understanding, Mr Oliver, not coldness and bullying.'

'And you understand my children better than I do?' he sneered.

'At least I understand that they need affection! You just ignore them. You won't even take them up in your precious helicopter!'

'Children have no place in a helicopter,' Blaize replied stiffly. 'Especially not Terry. He's too young. Once they're older, then of course they'll come with me.'

'The reason Tracey is doing badly at school is because she needs more love and understanding from *you*. She worships you, can't you see that? You could make her study every hour that God sent, and it still wouldn't help as much as a minute's quiet talk.'

'Tracey is lazy and rebellious. Like her mother, she has been spoiled more than is good for her.'

'Spoiled? A girl who's already had to see a child psychologist?'

'Ah.' His mouth twisted. 'You really have been digging in the dirt, haven't you?'

'A child's problems are not *dirt*,' she gritted. 'And I didn't find that out from Tracey.'

'From dear Jason, then?'

'As it happens, yes. But there's no use in talking to you,' Leila said, brushing tears away from her cheeks with her wrists. 'Your mind is as closed as your heart.'

Blaize's eyes dropped involuntarily to the dark spots on her skin where bruises were already starting to form. 'Well, there's certainly no use in talking nonsense,' he said shortly.

She took an unsteady breath. 'I don't see any point in my staying here any longer, Mr Oliver. My presence has obviously been a disruption from the very start. There are plenty of others to take my place, who won't give you nearly as much trouble.' She turned away from him, reaching for her bathrobe. 'I'll go back to London as soon as there's an available flight. You can tell Carol exactly what you want to. It doesn't matter to me.'

He stood in silence for a moment. When he spoke again, his voice was quieter. 'There's no question of your leaving me until your replacement arrives. This is a crucial time. I'm flying to Gerona tomorrow morning, for a meeting with some important people in the Catalan clothing industry. I need you there.'

'You should have thought of that before you came barging in here with your abuse and your insults.'

'You're coming with me tomorrow!'

'And you expect me to jump to your command?' she said over her shoulder. 'After the way you've just treated me?'

'I expect you to fulfil your obligations.' He turned her round and looked into her eyes hotly. 'And don't kid yourself about my influence. A word from me, and Carol would drop you like a hot potato.'

'Threats?' she asked drily, and smiled with a mouth like a bruised rose-petal. 'You're excelling yourself tonight, Mr Oliver.'

'I'm not threatening you.'

'Yes, you are.' She looked up at him. 'I could almost feel sorry for you, if you weren't such a tyrant. You get so angry when things don't go exactly as you want them to. It must be very frustrating for a man like you to come across people who won't do precisely as you say, mustn't it?'

'I only expect them to do as I say when I pay their wages,' he said quietly. 'And I'll be the one to decide whether you go back to London, not you. You're too damned fond of a cop-out by half.'

'A cop-out?' she repeated haughtily.

'It's obvious why you prefer agency work,' he said contemptuously. 'So you've got an out, whenever you need one. Which must be pretty often. Your stock response to any problem is to announce that you're going home. Is that what you used to do as a little girl? Snatch up your toys and announce that you weren't playing any more?'

'We didn't have too many toys—in the gutter,' she said cuttingly.

He smiled without warmth. 'How long would you last in a regular job, Leila?'

'In your employment, about a week,' she retorted smartly. 'How long did your last personal assistant stick it out?'

'Five years,' he said in a hard voice.

'Before she left to join a convent, I imagine.'

'What do you mean, a convent?'

'Because she must have been a saint. Now, will you please get out of my bathroom and leave me in peace?'

Blaize stared at her bleakly for a moment. 'How can someone who looks like you be so disruptive?' he asked quietly. 'I don't know what you're doing to me and my family, Leila, but I don't like it.'

He turned and walked out. She heard her door slam, and sank against the wall tiredly.

What in heaven's name had happened with Tracey? Had the girl pulled some kind of performance out of her repertoire, specifically to stir up trouble between Leila and her father? Leila knew she had the acting skills to do it. Yet somehow she couldn't bring herself to believe that Tracey was capable of such treachery after the warm friendship they'd experienced today and this evening. Not unless Tracey had fooled her with truly malicious expertise.

What, then? Had Katherine egged her on to something she wouldn't normally have thought of? Katherine had obviously told Blaize a highly embroidered version of her own quarrel with Leila, and would probably do anything to hit back.

It hardly mattered, anyway.

Wearily, Leila got into her nightie and sank between the sheets. She shouldn't have let him bulldoze her into staying on here. She should have told him that wild horses wouldn't have kept her here.

Hell! The way he'd treated her, she had every right in the world to walk out. She would just need to tell Carol about the way he'd barged into her bathroom, and Carol would understand everything.

Why had she let him intimidate her? Blaize was terrifying when he was angry like that. Those eyes of his... When he had stared at her naked body, she'd had a moment of real fear. She'd almost thought he would drag her to the bed, throw her down, and——

She rolled on to her stomach, shutting out the image. She was angry with herself now—angry for having given way to her passion, and shown him so much naked emotion. She should have had more control. That made twice she'd slapped his face in two days.

He had stripped her tonight, seen her naked in more senses than one. She felt bruised, both internally and externally. That crack about coming from the gutter—how could he be so cruel, so brutal? Didn't he know how much she really cared about him? He'd degraded himself, as well as her, when he'd said that.

Their shared experience ought to have drawn them together. Instead, it seemed to have pushed them apart, brought them to even more fiercely opposed confrontations. Nothing seemed to explain why he was so antagonistic towards her.

Why? What kept going wrong between them? What factor poisoned their relationship? She'd never known anyone like Blaize. He affected her more than she knew how to deal with. Even when he hurt her, when his words cut deep into the most vulnerable parts of her mind, she could not stop caring for him, could not stop her heart from yearning for him, like a silly, romantic girl's.

Was she falling in love with him?

Could she really be falling in love with a man who, even if she had let him possess her body when he'd wanted to, would not dream of being serious about her?

'Falling in love.' What a stupid phrase. As though love were a hole in the ground, something you tripped into by accident, and then struggled to get out of. Or was that really an accurate simile, after all?

In some situations, love *was* a hole. It was a trap into which a woman could stumble, half-unwitting, and find herself enmeshed in the toils of a passion she had no way of controlling.

How long had she been here at Cap Sa Sal? She added the days up, and found to her faint surprise that she had already been here over three weeks. Not very much time to grow so hooked on a man. Not very much time left in which to unhook herself.

In another three weeks, her spell here would end, and then she would be heading back to London.

Leaving the pain and the confusion behind her. Leaving Blaize Oliver, and his children. Leaving a world that she'd never been meant to step into, had only been meant to keep on the fringes of. Like a child peering into a shop window at Christmas time.

The gutter. Such an ugly, brutal way of putting it. Telling her so finally that her interference was not wanted. Telling her exactly where her place was.

Her pillow was damp. She'd hardly been aware of her own tears, but they had been flowing nevertheless— flowing for herself, for Blaize, for the two children who had found such a tender place in her heart...

Emotional exhaustion brought sleep, unexpectedly, pulling the shutters down over her mind...

CHAPTER SEVEN

BREAKFAST the next morning was a strained affair. Katherine had left the night before, to go back to her own villa, but her presence was still very much in the air.

Blaize, wearing a beautiful charcoal silk suit, ate in silence, intently reading the business newspapers over his coffee. He hardly seemed to notice Leila's presence, which was crueller than any rudeness could have been.

Tracey sat next to him, pale and silent. She looked very much as though she hadn't slept last night. She kept her suspiciously red eyes on her plate. Leila's heart went out to her. She longed to go across and hug her, and ask her what had made her cry so bitterly last night. But she knew better than to meet her eyes. Blaize had forbidden her to have any more contact with his children, and if that was what he wanted, then so be it. She had learned her lesson at last.

Jason, who was leaving for England later that evening, did not come down for breakfast—whether he'd overslept, or was diplomatically keeping out of the way, Leila could not guess.

Only Terry, out of bed for the first time, as a special treat, seemed at all cheerful, and unaware of the heavy atmosphere. Wrapped in his dressing-gown, he sat next to Lucy, who wore a distinctly uncomfortable expression, as though she, too, had received the brunt of Blaize's displeasure last night.

It didn't help that Terry prattled happily to Leila right through breakfast, making no secret of his affection for her. Hard as it was to answer him in monosyllables, Leila tried her best, but with the exuberance of a nine-year-old who was feeling much better, he seemed not to notice her efforts to snub him.

It was Tracey, in the end, who got out of her chair and leant over him. 'Come on,' she ordered in a motherly tone, 'you've been out of bed long enough. Let Lucy take you up now.'

Reluctantly, Terry allowed himself to be conducted back to his room, demanding to know why he couldn't kiss Leila.

Blaize glanced at his watch.

'We've got half an hour,' he said briefly, looking across at Leila. 'Rick will be waiting at the helicopter at nine. In the meantime, I want you to look over this.' He passed her a sheaf of notes, some of the passages ringed with a thick red pencil. 'Just read the marked bits. It's part of a general report on the clothing industry in northern Spain. It'll help you have some idea what's going on this morning.'

'Yes, Mr Oliver,' she said, pulling the notes towards her.

'You're ostensibly taking notes this morning,' he said in an impersonal voice as they drove out to the chopper, half an hour later. 'I want a formal record of this meeting. They want me to see a presentation about their product, with a view to getting serious negotiations started when I get back to London, and, if things go well, we'll probably need a signed statement expressing our preliminary intentions. But I want you to keep your eyes and ears open in all senses. The people we're dealing with are clever businessmen. They're Catalans, which means they're shrewd and hard-headed, and I don't want to miss any nuances.'

'I'll do my best,' Leila said, nodding.

'Everything will be in English this morning, so you needn't worry about that. You've grasped the main points from the notes I gave you?'

'I think so.'

Leila had never flown in a helicopter before. The black machine, with its smoked-perspex canopy, was standing in a field half a mile from the house. As Blaize pulled up in the car, the rotors were already turning. Leila hunched instinctively as the buffeting wind swept across her. She felt Blaize's hand take her arm, leading her under the whirling thunder of the blades, helping her up the steps into the cockpit. Rick was waiting inside, wearing a pair of headphones, which he passed to Blaize.

It was Blaize who took the controls. While he made the pre-flight checks, Rick helped Leila strap herself into her seat, and gave her a set of ear-defenders to put on. She hugged her briefcase, which contained the slim portable Olivetti typewriter, among other things, and tried to restore some order to her tumbled blonde hair with one hand. Thank heaven she'd had the sense to get those long tresses cut before she'd come out to Spain, or she'd have been in one hell of a mess by now. She was wearing a simple grey suit with a silk blouse—every inch the proficient English secretary, cold and distantly forbidding. Well, she needed some kind of shield for her torn emotions, didn't she?

Leila's stomach lurched as the helicopter surged upwards and banked over the field, and then they were soaring over the countryside in the direction of Gerona.

The scheduled meeting turned out, in fact, to be two meetings. The first took place at the factory, an impressively modern fashion-house in the industrial sector of the city, equipped with all the latest computer-guided machinery; and, after a brief coffee-break, they all moved to a smart hotel in the charming Old Town, near the great cathedral, where the clothing people had rented a conference suite.

Apart from secretaries, the Spanish party consisted of four people in all—three men and a woman—working in highly professional shifts to present their proposals to Blaize Oliver. The basic premise was that he should use an existing chain of shops which he owned in the southern counties of the UK to market a new range of sports and leisure-wear called LaMotta, a rapidly growing concern that was jointly owned by the four young people; but the ramifications were endless, and the Spanish case was both complex and prolonged.

Leila was acutely aware of Blaize's isolation as he faced these four highly geared young businesspeople. How he must miss his personal assistant! Her own presence here at his side was no kind of substitute for a real advisor, someone who had enough of a grasp of the ins and outs of his businesses to be able to take a real part in the discussion.

Not that Blaize seemed to be finding it in any way hard to cope. He simply sat, watchful and brooding-eyed, listening to the presentation, and asking a quiet question from time to time.

There was a mountain of paperwork, dealing with past and projected profits, which Blaize and she were given some time to study.

More interestingly, they also had a videotape prepared. A television set was wheeled into the conference-room where they'd been talking, and Blaize and Leila watched a very slick exposition of the merchandise that was on offer.

The film covered the factory in Gerona which manufactured the clothes, and which they had just visited, explaining some of the more advanced processes in greater detail. It then moved to a fashion show where tall and elegant models were showing off the latest designs, and ended with detailed shots of retail outlets in northern Spain and France. Enthusiastic customers were shown buying as many of the tracksuits, nylon jackets and casual clothes as the beaming sales assistants could handle. It was as professional a piece of publicity as she'd seen.

There were several samples of the actual clothing on hand, too, including some designs due to be released later in the autumn. Blaize passed them over to Leila for inspection without comment. She examined the stuff carefully, checking the stitching and cutting, trying to assess the overall design in terms of what an English public would buy.

'Here, you keep this, and this,' one of the Spanish businessmen beamed, heaping jackets and tracksuits into Leila's lap. 'Everyone in England will be wearing this stuff in six months' time, and you'll be ahead of the trend. You can tell everyone you were the first to wear LaMotta clothes!'

Blaize checked his watch at last. 'I'm ready for my lunch,' he said, rising. Four pairs of anxious eyes were fixed on his face, but he was giving nothing away. 'My secretary and I will go and find some place to eat for an hour or two. We'll get back to you in the afternoon. Shall we meet back here at, say, four-thirty?'

He and Leila left the hotel, and walked through the narrow, medieval streets towards the river. It was a charming old city, its mazes of winding streets occasionally opening out unexpectedly on to grandiose flights of stone steps, or leading in and out of little squares, dominated by churches which seemed over-huge for their locations. The shops along the way were resplendent with precious antiques, or elegant clothes, adding to the atmosphere of walking through some remote and glamorous past.

The place he took her to was called Jordi's, a very smart restaurant which overlooked the river.

A starchy-looking head waiter dissolved into an obliging jelly in the face of Blaize's commanding presence and fluent Spanish, and ushered them upstairs, to the more exclusive part of the restaurant.

The table they got was superb, secluded from the other diners, and right next to a huge window that opened out on a panorama of the river and the picturesque old multi-storied houses along its bank.

Leila sat opposite Blaize. It was the first private moment they'd had since last night's flaming row, and she felt uncomfortable enough to bury her face in the menu, rather than meet his eyes.

'Better stick to something you know,' he advised. 'Catalan food can be a little strange on English palates.'

'I'm not as insular as all that,' she replied evenly. 'I do occasionally deviate from sausages and mash.'

His eyes glittered. 'You take everything I say as an insult, don't you?'

'No, Mr Oliver, I just feel like something different,' she answered politely. 'What's *estofado de conejo*?'

'Meat stew,' he replied succinctly.

'Is it good?'

'I think it's delicious. But then, I'm evidently not as cosmopolitan in my tastes as you are.'

She resisted the impulse to make some retort. 'Then I'll have that, please. With a salad to start with.'

'I want a steak with pepper. Let's have a drink first. I need one, after this morning.'

'Oh...gin and tonic,' she decided, in answer to his enquiring eyebrow.

'A Bloody Mary for me.' He delivered the order to the hovering waiter, and leaned back, surveying her with those deep green eyes. 'What did you think of our friends this morning?'

'Very businesslike. Very enterprising.'

'I'll say.' Their drinks materialised, and Blaize cradled the long red glass in both competent hands before taking a first gulp. 'They're fast movers. I don't trust people who are in a hurry,' he said thoughtfully. 'Or am I just getting old?'

Leila made no comment, knowing she wasn't expected to make one. She drank another mouthful of gin, grimacing slightly as the rather sickly alcohol burned its way down.

'Something wrong with your gin?'

He didn't miss a damned thing! 'No, it's fine. I'm silly, though, I don't really feel like gin. I should have had a Bloody Mary instead.'

'Have mine. I don't mind gin.' Before she could protest, he had swapped the glasses round.

'Well—thank you, but you needn't have——' She fished a clean hanky out of her pocket. 'I've smudged lipstick on the rim, I'm afraid.' Stupidly, she was flushing as she erased the pink trace from the glass.

He watched her drily. 'I see you're back in your carefully neutral camouflage,' he commented. 'Beige eyeshadow, pale lipstick, formal suit. You positively blossomed on Saturday night, and now you're back in your shell.'

'I obviously blossomed more than was good for me,' she observed in a grey voice. There was no way of telling where *his* lips had touched the glass, and, for all she knew, she might now be drinking from the same place. The tomato-juice was refreshing, undercut with the clean tang of vodka. 'Mmm, that's better.'

'Add a drop of snake-venom, and call it a Bloody Leila,' he suggested, watching her. 'But you were telling me what you thought about the proposals we've been listening to all morning.'

She almost choked. 'Was I?'

'Indeed,' he nodded. 'You've got a brain in that blonde head. You must have some comment to make.'

'How about—this is a rapid-turnover situation of high leverage potential, underpinned by short-term factoring and a strong customer-preferential retail base with built-in analogue input-output differentials?'

He couldn't help breaking in a grin at her wicked parody. It was like the sunshine pouring in through stormclouds. 'OK, there was a lot of waffle. What about the underlying concept?'

'Mr Oliver, you don't really want my opinion on a subject like this?'

'My dear Miss Thomas, I do,' he contradicted calmly. 'I have to give these gentlemen some kind of reply over the next few days. If I say yes, they'll be committed to some important, and expensive, preliminary steps. If I say no, I might be turning down a very profitable venture.' He finished off her gin. 'You have strong opinions on everything in your vicinity, from the way I bring up my children to what you're having for your lunch. What's your opinion on this matter?'

'Well . . . I liked the clothes.'

'Go on.'

'The colours were good, with unusual combinations. There's a distinctive stamp to them that's very nice. And the designs were just the sort of thing people like— comfortable, but not inelegant.' She reached under the table, and pulled out one of the tracksuits she'd been presented with. 'The material is good quality. And these colours are very fashionable this year.'

He tested the material between finger and thumb. 'Will people buy this kind of thing?'

'No question. I've seen a lot of people wearing this sort of thing already. Not just jogging, either. You could wear this round the house, and not be embarrassed if someone dropped in.'

'What is this, some synthetic?'

'A kind of polyester.' She nodded. 'It should last well enough. If you're interested in their offer, we can take these things home today, and put them through half a dozen washes before you go back to England. That'll show whether the dyes are good, and whether the material goes out of shape in any way.'

He glanced up at her. 'So you're in favour of getting this thing off the ground?'

'I didn't say that,' she corrected him quickly. 'I only said I liked the product.'

He held her gaze for a moment, but he wasn't seeing her. He was thinking so hard she could almost see the wheels of his mind turning. Then he shrugged. 'All right. I'll let them get going.'

'Not on *my* say-so?' she gasped.

'They're committed to far more expense than we are during the initial phase,' he answered obliquely. 'This afternoon we'll discuss the terms of a preliminary contract, to go to our mutual legal departments for checking. We'll make sure there's a get-out clause, in case we don't like the way things pan out.' He lifted a sardonic eyebrow at her. 'You can draw that up for me. Get-out clauses are your speciality, aren't they?'

'I should be able to think of something,' she replied thinly.

Their food arrived, and Leila sampled her stew, which appeared to consist of vegetables, dumplings, and chicken. It was delicious, full of flavour, and the meat was meltingly tender. 'Gosh, that's good,' she said, tucking in. 'The chicken is superb.'

'It's not chicken,' he informed her casually.

'Isn't it?' She chewed appreciatively. 'It tastes like chicken. What is it?'

'Rabbit.'

She swallowed her mouthful hastily, and stared at him. 'You're joking?'

'Why should I joke?' he enquired, evidently enjoying his own steak *au poivre*. 'It's usually very good. Have you any objection to eating a fluffy little bunny?'

'Oh, *don't*,' she mourned in protest. She stared at her plate, noticing the delicate ribs and slender bones for the first time. 'I've never eaten rabbit before! Why didn't you tell me?'

'You were so busy telling me what an adventurous eater you were,' he reminded her with a glint in his eyes. 'Anyway, you wanted something typically Spanish, didn't you?'

'But I love rabbits!'

'And you don't love sheep, pigs and cows?'

'They're different.' She stared at her plate. 'Rabbits are...cuddly.'

His expression was droll. 'Good lord. I would never have suspected you of such sentimentality. Is this the same Leila Thomas who spends her weekends slapping my face?'

'You should see the bruises on my arms.' She glared at him. 'And not telling me that *conejo* means rabbit was a low-down trick.'

'You city girls,' he sighed. 'Can't you eat it?'

'I don't think so. It's delicious, but when I think of a cuddly little rabbit with long ears and a twitchy nose——' She shuddered.

'Well, we've already swapped drinks...' He reached over and exchanged her plate for his. 'I'll take the cuddly little stew with the long ears and twitchy nose.'

The intimacy of the gesture moved her, even though the peppered steak was not what she would ideally have chosen. It was a fiery, masculine dish with enough peppercorns to make her tongue burn. But it was preferable to the meek flesh of her rabbit.

'Thank you for swapping. I hate wasting food.'

'So do I.' He nodded. 'It drives me mad to see Terry and Tracey leaving their meals half-finished. I suppose it's to do with the way we were brought up.'

'Oh, yes—in the gutter,' she put in sweetly.

'Put your claws back in,' he advised smokily. 'And don't keep throwing something at me that I said when I was angry.'

'But you meant it,' Leila rejoined, slicing the juicy piece of steak. 'There was a lot of bitterness behind that remark.'

'I've worked my whole life so that my children's lives could be different,' he said, those tiger's eyes gleaming at her. 'I didn't want them to know any of the things I knew. Poverty. Loneliness. Humiliation. Having to grow up without real parents. But I've already made one unforgivable mistake with them. I picked the wrong woman to be their mother, and made them go through the hell of a divorce. I don't want anything else to go wrong for my children, Leila. If that makes me overprotective with them, I'm sure you'll understand why.'

That was the closest thing to an apology she would ever hear from Blaize Oliver—of that she was certain! 'People do make mistakes,' Leila said carefully. 'Especially parents. Very few of them are really "unforgivable".'

'An unusually circumspect observation from the normally direct Miss Thomas,' Blaize remarked ironically. 'What are you getting at?'

She took a deep breath. 'Just that you shouldn't blame yourself for the divorce. Not if it wasn't your fault.'

'But it *was* my fault,' he said flatly. 'I allowed Vanessa's beauty and charm to blind me to her fundamental unfitness to be a mother. I wasn't exaggerating in what I told you a couple of weeks ago, Leila,' he added, his expression bitter. 'She doesn't have the faintest flicker of interest in her children. She wouldn't admit to anyone that she was even pregnant, you know. She hid it. She wasn't proud of motherhood; she was ashamed of it. She dieted like fury from the moment she knew she was expecting, to try and hide the bulge. She's the only woman I've known who actually *lost* weight during her pregnancies. Both times.' He shook his head grimly. His face had hardened while he'd been speaking, his eyes changing colour, like the sea. 'Heaven knows why I wasn't warned after Tracey. I suppose I thought she would show more interest in her second child. But Terry's arrival just made things worse.'

'But then you have nothing to reproach yourself with. It wasn't your fault.'

'They say history repeats itself,' Blaize said, and pushed his plate away, as though he'd lost his appetite. 'To a certain extent, that's happened with me. Instead of giving them a happy, stable home, I've already subjected them to a lot of pain that they should never had had to go through. I'd rather never marry again, rather never have another woman in the house, than put them through any more suffering.'

Leila sat in silence, picking at her steak. In the face of Blaize's passion, her own appetite had faded. Since that blazing row, she was just starting to appreciate exactly how much he loved his children. They meant all the world to him. Far from being a selfish and inconsiderate father, he cared too much, and felt their unhappiness all too keenly. She'd misjudged him badly on that score.

'You once told me you were constitutionally unable to trust women,' she said quietly. 'You meant that, didn't you?'

'Sure,' Blaize said, a shade too casually. 'I've had too many bad experiences with them to be much of a romantic. Mind if I smoke?'

'I didn't know you did. But of course, go ahead.'

'It's a rare vice, and one I indulge in only on special occasions.' He summoned the waiter, and ordered a cigar. Their half-finished meals were cleared away. They both declined a pudding, but, on Blaize's advice, Leila agreed to a Spanish brandy with her coffee. It came in a huge balloon glass, and was, as he had promised, unusually mild and palatable.

He lit his cigar with due ceremony, and blew a cloud of acrid smoke into the air, watching the curls and plumes with narrowed eyes.

She watched his face, aware of an odd feeling in her heart. How many emotions you've made me feel, she thought numbly. At times I've hated you, feared you, at times almost loved you. You're like no one I've ever known...

When she went away from here, he was going to leave a great big hole in her life. A hole that would probably be impossible to fill. She suddenly found herself cursing the luck that had ever carried her here, and had brought her into contact with someone who had been custom-made by some malign deity to affect her like this.

Because there could never be anyone like Blaize again. A man so overwhelmingly attractive, sharing so much of her own experience, yet so diametrically opposed to her in almost every way...

She had been born to love him. And he had been born to break her heart.

'You also once said you'd made some efforts to trace your parents,' Leila said, wanting to get away from her own dark thoughts. 'Would it be an intrusion if I asked what you found out? Or, at least, whether it made you any happier?'

'Miss Inquisitive, is it?' he rumbled forbiddingly.

'I've told you almost everything there is to know about myself,' Leila reminded him gently.

'So you did.' He was still watching the smoke, rather than her. 'What makes you want to know my secrets, Leila? Morbid curiosity?'

'Something more, I think,' she told him, her skin flushing slightly. 'But if you don't want to talk about it, I'll understand completely.'

'I've never told anyone. Never in my life.' The green eyes were on hers now, intent and dark. 'Why should I tell you?'

'I don't know,' she said in a small voice. 'Maybe because I'll understand.'

'Men don't always want to be understood,' he commented drily. But suddenly he was talking, his husky voice low and thoughtful. Talking about his childhood, telling her about his growing realisation during those long-ago days that he was not like other children in the little north country village where he'd been born.

Unlike Leila, his upbringing had been rural, rather than urban. 'I grew up in the context of a farming community,' he told her, his expression faraway. 'With deep, rustling woods, and hillsides that were covered with heather and gorse. With fields deep in snow, and little, crystal-clear rivers that were so cold they made your bones ache, even in summer.'

'It sounds beautiful,' she said.

'It was,' he smiled. 'It still is.'

For the first six years of his life he'd been fostered by a local farmer with a large family, and had gone to a village school, where he'd been happy—even though he'd learned to use his fists early.

'Children can be very cruel,' he commented wryly. 'Especially country children. They're more direct than city kids, and they pick up the facts of life earlier, and in a more earthy form. When they teased me about having no parents, I used to fight them. Until I learned that it was a better defence to invent stories.'

'What sort of stories?' she asked curiously.

He shrugged. 'Oh...I used to insist that I *did* have parents, but that they were far away. I used to say that my father was an aristocratic secret agent, working in some foreign country. And that my mother was a beautiful spy, too. I always claimed they'd come back for me one day.' He met her compassionate look with a slight smile. 'My foster-brothers and sisters used to listen, open-mouthed. And if they didn't believe me, they were too frightened of my temper to show it. But it got so that I almost believed my own inventions, in the end. It was a fantasy that I fell in love with. As I grew older, and moved from home to home, I elaborated it, added details, turned it into quite a soap opera. My fictitious parents became quite real to me, Leila.'

'It was a natural reaction,' she said gently. 'Sometimes I used to weave daydreams around my parents, too. I used to have fantasies about them coming to claim me.'

'Yes,' Blaize nodded, 'with some complicated but perfectly reasonable explanation for why they'd abandoned you. And you would forgive them.'

'You'd hug them and kiss them...'

'And they'd promise that they would never go away again...'

They were staring into each other's eyes now, as though hypnotised by the emotion they were sharing. She had never felt as close as this to another human being in her life.

It was Blaize who broke the spell. He knocked the ash off his cigar with a scornful smile. 'But there comes a time when the fantasies have to end, doesn't there?'

'Yes.' She nodded, looking down into her brandy. 'When did yours end?'

'On the day I went to find out the truth.' His voice had grown cold, remote. 'Like you, I made some enquiries. I was sixteen at the time, and getting to the stage where I was almost an adult. But not enough of an adult to know when to leave well enough alone. Not adult enough to know that fantasies are better than the truth, any day.'

He drained the brandy, and nodded to the waiter for another. 'My researches took me to Newcastle upon Tyne. To an area called Crowther, where I had an address. An address that might, or might not, be my mother's.' He looked up. 'Have you ever been to Newcastle?'

'I spent a couple of days there once, standing in for a typist. I remember a very elegant Georgian street called Grey Street, and a monument. But I didn't go to Crowther.'

He shook his head ironically. 'No. You wouldn't have done, a nice girl like you. Over the past twenty years, Crowther has improved out of all recognition. It's still grim. But then it was rough, Leila. A place you didn't go to unless you had a very good reason. The moment I got off the bus, I knew that my dreams of an aristocratic, romantic background were over.'

Leila wanted to reach out and touch him, but she didn't dare. She sat without moving, just watching his taut face.

'The first address I had was a blank. The bird had flown, years before. But the woman next door had another address for me, a few streets away. So I went there.' His mouth tightened. 'It was even shabbier, a place that had shed all pretence of dignity. I couldn't believe that my mother had ever lived in places like these. Anyway, she wasn't there, either. Again, there was a woman next door. A woman in the same line of business as the last one.' He glanced at Leila. 'By then, of course, I was starting to realise what sort of woman my mother was, and what she did for a living.'

'Oh, Blaize,' Leila said, with a little moan of grief for him.

He went on in a flat monotone. 'The third address was the right one. She lived in an apartment block that was slightly better than the other two I'd visited. She was clearly doing well in her profession. There was even a touch of glamour. The place was almost inviting—all pink plush and velvet curtains, and a view, right over the river. The location was clearly convenient for the factories and the dockyards and the pubs. The places where she could meet her clients.' He gave Leila a cold smile, but he wasn't looking at her any more. He was looking into himself, into his own past. 'Her clients,' he repeated, in a softer voice. 'That's who she thought I was, at first. One of her clients.'

She closed her eyes in pain, his words washing over her like icy water.

'Like you, I had a moment of instant recognition when she opened the door. It was the event I'd dreamed of for so long—recognising my own features in the face of another human being. Recognising my mother. I couldn't believe how young she was! She might have been my sister, rather than my mother. And she was smiling, as though she recognised me. Except that recognising strange men was just one of the tricks of trade.' Blaize laughed softly. 'She said she couldn't quite remember my name, but that she never forgot a face.'

'Did you—did you tell her who you were?'

'I was waiting for her to recognise me,' Blaize answered. 'I couldn't take my eyes off her. She had that blank, exhausted look that so many women in her profession get. But, beneath it, she was still beautiful; you could see that.'

Yes, she would have had to have been beautiful, Leila reflected, to have a son like Blaize. 'Was she like you?'

Blaize took out his wallet, and opened it. There was a photograph in an inside flap. He took it out and passed it over to Leila. 'I stole that from her. It was on a sideboard, in a little frame. She can't have been much older than that when she had me.'

Leila stared at the beautiful, oval face. You couldn't tell the colouring from the black and white photograph, which had obviously been taken some years before, but the features of the eighteen or nineteen-year-old girl were exquisite. The only thing that marred the tranquil beauty of the face was a sadness in the eyes, and on the full mouth. A sadness that seemed to reach out of the picture and touch Leila's heart.

'She's lovely.' Leila looked up at Blaize. 'If you had to steal this from her, then you can't have told her who you were.'

'It would have been cruel, at that moment,' Blaize replied. 'You see, she'd invited me in, and was talking to me as though I were there for...' He grimaced. 'For her services.'

'But that's horrible,' Leila mourned. 'You must have been in a state of shock.'

'I was numb, more than anything else. The pain only came later. It wasn't hard to tell what her problem was, Leila. She never stopped drinking while I was there, re-filling her glass before it even got half-empty. I think it was the drink that stopped her from realising who I was. I like to think that, anyway.'

'Blaize,' she said quietly, 'I'm so terribly sorry. I don't know what to say. What you went through was far worse than what happened to me...'

'I don't know.' Unexpectedly, his fingers were lacing through hers, warm and strong. 'I had a shock to my delusions. But you had a rejection. That's far worse. I don't know how you survived that, as a person.' Deep green eyes held hers, without challenge or anger for once, just with compassion and tenderness. 'I don't think I could have survived it, Leila.'

'Oh, I'm sure you could,' she said with a broken little laugh. His fingers tightened round hers. 'I can see now why you've never told anyone this, Blaize. But you know that I understand, don't you?'

'I think you do.' He nodded. 'Sometimes I think you understand everything about me.'

The quiet words hung in the air for a long while, drifting with the curls of cigar-smoke. Then Blaize drew back, staring out of the window at the river. 'In the end, she got impatient with this skinny kid who sat staring at her like a ghost, paralysed and speechless. She said she would wait for me in the bedroom.'

Leila winced.

'When she was gone, I stole the photograph you're looking at. I left money on the table, everything I had, and just fled. What else could I do?'

'Nothing,' Leila said softly.

'Nothing,' he echoed. 'Not then, anyway. Later, when I was a man, I was able to do more.'

'You sent her money?'

'I had to be very careful.' Blaize nodded. 'I didn't want her to know where it was coming from. I told my lawyers to get in touch with her, and tell her that a distant relation in Devon had died. Why Devon?' He smiled. 'I wanted to get her away from Crowther, and out of the profession she was in. There had been pictures of Devon on the walls, so I guessed that she had a dream of going there. Anyway, the "legacy" consisted of a cottage near the sea, in a very pretty little town, and a life-income that effectively made her a well-off woman.'

'That was generous of you.'

'Generous?' His expression was bitter. 'How old is the girl in that picture, Leila?'

'Eighteen? Nineteen at the most?'

'I reckon she was eighteen when that was taken. And she had already borne me by then.'

'How do you know?' Leila asked curiously.

'I can see it in her eyes. She'd already had me, and lost me.'

Leila stared at the picture, and felt her heart constrict. Yes. That was why sorrow lived in the lovely eyes and mouth. Blaize was right.

'Something must have put a girl like that on the road she ended up on. She wouldn't have chosen it willingly. It was my fault, Leila.'

'What are you saying?'

'She ended up the way she did because of having an illegitimate child. Me.' There was pain in his face, an echo of the pain in the photograph.

'How can you say that?' she gasped.

'You don't know what those little village communities are like. I do. They'd never have forgiven her for having an illegitimate child. She probably fell for some married man, some local swine who seduced her and abandoned her, and ruined her life. I don't even want to know who he is. There's no question in my mind, Leila. It was my arrival that destroyed my mother's prospects. I owed her a life.'

'Oh, Blaize! Have you tormented yourself with that, all your life?'

'I've tried to make reparations.' He took back the picture, and put it carefully back in his wallet. 'She still lives in that cottage. The annuity which mysterious old ''uncle'' left her has a strange way of growing. By now, she's quite a wealthy woman, and highly respected by everyone in the village.' There was a glint of humour in his eyes. 'It's rather a posh little place, but not a soul in the town suspects that Mrs Oliver, with the Jaguar and the diamonds, was once a lady of the night, in a slum in Crowther.'

'And she still doesn't know who you are?'

Blaize shook his head slightly. 'No. And no one in my family even suspects that I have a mother. Not even my lawyers know who she is. I've never told a soul.'

'Not even Vanessa?'

'Vanessa?' he snorted in contempt. 'If I'd told Vanessa about my mother she'd have had a nervous breakdown. No, you're the first living soul I've ever told.'

Leila was silent for a while, emotion forming a lump in her throat. 'I appreciate that,' she said quietly, at last. 'But wouldn't it be better——?'

'To reveal all?' Blaize finished for her, his expression ironic. 'Tell my mother that her wealth comes from her long-lost, illegitimate son? Tell Tracey and Terry that their granny is alive, after all, and have to explain why I've kept it a secret all these years? Explain to Katherine that she's going to have a mother-in-law, after all? Turn everybody's life upside-down, including my own?' He shook his head, the cigar smoking unheeded between his fingers. 'No, Leila. Things are better off the way they are.'

'But—your mother doesn't even know whether you're alive or dead. It might make all the difference to her to know that you've become so successful, and that you care about her!'

'Now you're talking the kind of sentimental nonsense that Katherine likes to indulge in,' he said drily. 'I'm pretty sure my mother knows where I am, and what my life has become.'

'Are you?' She blinked.

'I traced her.' He shrugged. 'If she'd ever had the impulse, it would have been equally easy for her to have traced me. I'm sure she'll have done it.'

'In which case,' Leila said gently, 'she'll be very, very proud of you.'

'Maybe. But she's never been in contact.'

'So you both know about the other... but she doesn't imagine that you're supporting her?'

'Yes. And that's the way I want it. To let her know that she's been living on my money for the past twenty years, when she probably has a huge guilt complex about me, would not be exactly diplomatic. Nor would it be exactly diplomatic to intrude in her life, if she wants to hide what she was from me. It might spoil all the happiness she's managed to build up since I got her out of Crowther. No, little one. It's enough for me to know that she's alive, and as happy as possible. I don't want to intrude into her life after all these years.'

She watched his face with gentle eyes. 'You're a very strange man,' she said softly.

'And you're a very strange woman. Strange, and dangerous. How the hell did you worm all that out of me?' His face was changing as he spoke, the shutters coming down. Every line of his grim expression showed her that he was now regretting having opened his heart to her. 'I must have been mad, telling you all that.'

'Of course you weren't mad!'

'No? Haven't I just put myself in your power?' His passionate mouth twisted. 'If you wanted to, you could use that information against me to very good effect. A little scandal about Blaize Oliver would be worth a lot of money in the City.'

'Blaize!'

'Oh, I'd pay a small fortune to stop it getting around,' he said drily. 'Not for my own sake, of course. But for the sake of protecting Terry and Tracey, and my mother...' He looked at her darkly. 'How do I know you won't go straight off to Fleet Street with the tale, once your six weeks with me is up?'

'I can't believe that you'd think that of me!' She was so wounded by his lack of trust in her that she was stunned. 'I'm not like that!'

'Everyone's like that,' he retorted shortly. 'And, as I told you, I especially don't trust women.'

'You have to trust someone now and then,' she said in a low, urgent voice. 'Don't regret telling me about your mother, Blaize. I'm not going to use it against you! It's as sacred to me as...as my own past.' She held his eyes. 'You're the only person who knows about *me*, remember. I've never told anyone else, either.'

Blaize met her eyes for a moment. He nodded slightly, as though considering what she had said. 'I don't regret telling you, Leila. I'd rather have told you than anyone else in my life. But I'll never tell another living soul. Not even Katherine, when we get married. I don't want her to know.'

Abruptly, he leaned forward and crushed the cigar into the ashtray.

'I thought you weren't meant to do that with a good cigar,' she heard herself saying, her voice almost normal.

'When we get married.' The words were echoing through her mind like a leaden bell. So he was going to marry Katherine, after all. The pain swelled inside her, threatening to burst into helpless tears.

'You aren't. But nobody can obey all the rules all the time.' He summoned the waiter impatiently, then rose to his feet. 'Come on,' he said harshly. 'We've got to get back to the LaMotta people by four-thirty, and we have some documents to draft. You look as though you're going to burst into tears at any moment. Don't be a sentimental fool, Leila. We're here on business, remember?'

As they flew back to Cap Sa Sal in the late afternoon sunlight, Leila's mind was throbbing with thoughts of Blaize. So much was now clear to her, so much that had been almost impossible to understand before. The things he'd told her about his life had suddenly made it all click into place. Why he behaved the way he did with women, for one thing. It was little wonder that he found it so hard to trust them.

For another thing, she understood for the first time just how deeply he dreaded rejection. After discovering what his mother was, after what Vanessa had done to him, it was far easier to stay uninvolved, to keep his relationships to casual affairs, than to risk more pain. It was one of the keys to his character, she was sure of that! Somewhere deep in his psyche, he felt he had to compensate by being better than others, because of his birth. It was something she could understand. Her own reaction to being illegitimate had been different, but then, she was not a man. And her life had been much easier than his, she understood that.

That explained the flame that always burned in him, the need to excel, and achieve more than others. And it explained why he was so protective of his children, why he had turned on her so furiously when he'd thought she had hurt Tracey.

Yet, for all the hardship he had had to bear, he was so good to others. Even his treatment of his mother had shown the utmost tact and consideration. He was a man who did good to others, and cared deeply for those who mattered to him. And he asked little in return.

Leila stared out unseeingly at the green landscape of Catalonia, rushing by beneath them. She perceived now that her feelings for Blaize Oliver went much deeper than she could ever have imagined. She'd known him a bare three weeks, and he was already a part of her life, something so intrinsic to her being that she didn't know how she was ever going to be able to leave him.

How would she manage without him? She glanced at his face as he concentrated on flying the helicopter, both tanned hands on the controls, dark glasses shading his eyes. For the first time in her life, for the first time ever, she had felt that she *belonged*. Belonged to Blaize Oliver, the only man she could ever truly be at one with.

And Blaize was going to marry Katherine Henessey. He was lost to her. He had been lost to her from the start. Men like Blaize didn't get serious about girls like Leila. His whole career had been a search for wealth and stability. How could he ever love a woman who came from the very kind of background that he had been escaping from all his life?

It was time to start cauterising the feelings in her heart. Burning them out before the ultimate pain of leaving tore her apart...

They landed in the same field, where Blaize gave the controls over to Rick. He and Leila got out, watched Rick take off again to fly the chopper back to its hangar, then drove up to the house in the car. It had been a long, tiring day, and they said little to one another.

When they got back to the house, Jason Tennant, the last of the weekend guests, was preparing to leave in a couple of hours. Relations between him and Blaize were still slightly stiff, and Leila had a brief drink in their company before taking herself off upstairs, guessing that her presence would not be helping to ease the atmosphere.

She was just about to drop in on Terry when she remembered Blaize's injunction of last night, that she should stay away from the kids. Presumably that still stood, despite what had passed between them this afternoon.

Anyway, it was better this way. It was time to start curtailing her feelings for the children, too. She didn't want her heart to be broken into three different pieces when she had to leave...

She walked past the children's rooms, fighting down the urge to go in and see them, and only gave way to her feelings when she was in the privacy of her own room.

She showered and changed, then lay on her bed, closing her eyes. A little sleep before dinner might not go amiss. Exhaustion would only make the danger of breaking down all the more hard to withstand.

CHAPTER EIGHT

BUT Leila didn't sleep for very long. The knock that awoke her after about an hour was Jason's.

'I just wanted a little chat,' he told her as she opened the door. 'I'm driving to the airport straight after dinner and it's a little difficult to talk, with Blaize in his present mood.'

'Is he still hostile towards you?'

'Only when you're around,' Jason said drily. 'It seems you and he have pulled off some fantastic coup this afternoon. But he's like a bear with a sore head whenever you and I are in the same room.'

'Come in,' she invited with a sigh. There were two armchairs in her room, and they sat down in them. The evening sky was violet-blue outside the windows, a cool breeze starting to lift the oppressive summer heat of the day.

'This hasn't been a very pleasant break for you,' she said guiltily, 'and it's all been my fault.'

'Nonsense. Anyway, there'll be other weekends.' His shrewd brown eyes assessed her pale face. 'You don't look too happy yourself, Leila. Are you all right?'

'Just a little tired.'

'Blaize is obviously overworking you,' he said disapprovingly. 'That's a symptom of his high regard, by the way. He only slave-drives the people he really respects.'

'I doubt whether Blaize respects me,' Leila rejoined, shaking her head.

'Oh, you're the best thing since sliced bread.' Jason smiled. 'I've never heard him so enthusiastic about anyone. He's just been telling me how bright and perceptive you are. He thinks all the world of you. The best secretary he's ever had, in fact.' He looked at her downturned face. 'You don't look very pleased to hear that.'

'Oh, I am,' she said, rousing herself with an effort. 'I like to think I'm doing my job well.'

An efficient secretary. That was all she was to him.

'I can see the feelings are reciprocal,' Jason said in a softer voice. 'Though, in your case perhaps they go a little deeper. Am I right?'

'Oh, he's a super boss,' she said with a bright smile. But her false cheerfulness didn't fool Jason.

'Leila, Leila,' he sighed. 'You haven't fallen in love with him, have you?'

'Of course not!'

But he hadn't missed the way her eyes were suddenly wet, either. 'Damn,' he said softly. 'I'd give anything to stop you from being hurt, Leila. But I'm afraid you're going to be.' He leaned forward to lay his hand over hers. 'Blaize is going to marry Katherine Henessey,' he told her gently but firmly. 'I've been speaking to Katherine today. They've already set the date, in fact. She's downstairs with Blaize now, discussing it. No matter how much he respects you as an employee, it doesn't go deeper than that. It never could.'

'I know,' she said tightly.

He was silent for a long time, giving her space in which to wrest back control of her emotions. 'Blaize Oliver isn't the only man in the world,' he said at last, looking out of the window. 'There are other people, maybe not too far away from here, who feel very strongly about you . . .'

She shook her head in mute answer to his words. She could never love Jason. She could never love any other man, not after Blaize. 'I'm sorry, Jason,' she whispered. 'Truly, I am.'

'So am I,' he said heavily. 'It seems both of us are in the same sort of fix.' He heaved himself upright, as though his big frame were suddenly too heavy. 'Are you coming down to dinner?'

'I don't think so.' The thought of being with Blaize and Katherine and the children at the same table was unbearable. 'I'm—I'm not too hungry, I think I'll skip dinner.'

He looked down at her. 'Well, so long, Leila. I hope I'll see you again, soon. Do I get a goodbye kiss?'

She gave him one, on the cheek, and he grimaced wryly at the cool salutation.

'Take care.'

'You too.'

He walked out, leaving her to her solitude and grief.

There was another knock at her door, hours later. She emerged from her book to call, 'Come in!'

It was Tracey, looking very timid, and carrying a tray.

'I thought you might be hungry,' she said, putting the food down. 'You weren't at dinner...'

'Oh, Tracey!' She couldn't stop herself from hugging the girl. 'That was a very sweet thought.'

Tracey clung to her as though she were a rock in a stormy sea, and Leila realised she was crying. Poor child, she thought with a lump in her throat. How we adults make you suffer...

'I can't stay long,' Tracey sniffled. 'If Katherine knows I'm up here, she'll throw a fit. She thinks I'm taking this food to Terry.'

'And what will Terry do for his dinner?' Leila asked with a smile.

'I'll take him something else, later, when the coast's clear. He knows what I'm doing, and he doesn't mind waiting a bit for his dinner.'

Leila touched the girl's cheek. 'I'm sorry things have turned out so miserably, Tracey.'

'It's not your fault. It's Katherine.' Tracey's pretty mouth quivered as she said the name. 'She's the one who made Dad tell you to keep away from us.'

'Did she? That doesn't surprise me,' Leila said quietly.

'I used to think she was so wonderful. But she's not. She's evil.'

'Don't say that!'

'She is! And now Dad's going to marry her.' A distant door opened, and Tracey jumped to her feet in alarm. 'I wish he was going to marry you,' she said, in a broken voice. 'I thought you were going to make us unhappy, but you're the only one who really loves us—all of us!'

Before Leila could answer, Tracey had hurried out of the room.

The doctor pronounced Terry finally over his measles after his visit on Thursday. That evening, Blaize announced that he was taking Terry and Tracey on a trip up to the mountains on the weekend.

Katherine, to Leila's rather bitter amusement, angled in vain for an invitation to accompany them on the trip. Blaize was determined that this should be an outing just for the three of them, and he gently but firmly turned down Katherine's heavy hints.

That, in turn, made Katherine all the more spiteful towards Leila.

For the past week, Leila had been as quiet and humble as she knew how to be. She'd immersed herself in her work, had kept clear of the children, despite her aching heart, and had behaved towards Blaize with all the respect and distance due to an employer from his secretary.

She had also done her best to keep out of Katherine Henessey's way. Not satisfied with her victory over the weekend, Katherine liked to rub Leila's nose in her humiliation, never missing a chance to drop some cutting remark, never missing an opportunity to give Leila some unpleasant little task that emphasised her lowly position and confirmed Katherine's own place as mistress of Blaize's household.

'You don't mind checking all the linen for me?' she'd suggested. 'With all those guests, everything's in such a muddle. Mrs Saunders is so old that I'm thinking of retiring her, and one can't trust the housemaids, and you have such an orderly mind...'

Leila knew that if she'd complained to Blaize about the jobs Katherine gave her, she could have got out of doing them. But she preferred to spend two hours checking the linen, or whatever else Katherine commanded, and keeping Katherine happy, rather than risk another row, with its inevitable effect on the children.

Katherine, she had long since realised, was an expert at using the children as a lever to get what she wanted. That was why she was always so attentive towards them, because she knew that they were the key to Blaize's trust.

She had obviously made an especial attempt to get close to Tracey, but Leila had noticed that Tracey's slavish adoration of the older woman seemed to have faded over the past week. There was no answering warmth in her towards Katherine any more, and, though the teenager hardly spoke to Leila—at least when there was anyone to overhear—she was even cooler towards Katherine, to the point that Katherine grew snappy with her.

The atmosphere was growing heavier and more ominous by the day. It was almost a relief when Blaize and the children left for the mountains on Friday morning, and Katherine went back to her villa, leaving Leila with the rest of the staff to spend the weekend in peace.

She'd finished all the typing on their schedule by Saturday lunchtime. In the afternoon, she plugged the extension phones in by the poolside, and spent a deliciously lazy afternoon with Lucy, the governess, just sunbathing, swimming and dozing.

Sunday went much the same way. They had the great house all to themselves, and it was pleasant to feel her taut nerves unwind, free of both Katherine's nagging malice and Blaize's potent effect on her.

Except that she was already missing him. Wondering what he was doing. Wondering whether he was thinking of her, as she was thinking of him . . .

They weren't back by dinnertime, and had obviously decided to spend another night in the mountains. It would be bliss, Leila knew, for the children to be alone with just their father for a change. A real family outing, for once in their lives.

But she couldn't help the pain of missing him from swelling inside her, and she longed for his return. Was everything really all right? Perhaps there had been an accident, perhaps . . .

She dismissed her stupid fantasies impatiently.

She and Lucy watched television after dinner. They couldn't make much of the Spanish film that was on, nor of the sport on the other channels, and Leila ended up going to bed early.

Her sleep was restless and uneasy, filled with the sound of Blaize's voice and the image of his face. Some hours later, she surfaced again, as if sensing a presence beside her bed.

It was long after midnight. She rolled over drowsily. 'Hmm?'

'I didn't mean to wake you,' a deep voice said softly.

'Blaize?' she questioned, sitting up in bed to face him.

'Don't shout,' he hushed her, reaching out to touch her lips with his fingers. 'You'll wake the whole house up.'

'What time is it?'

'One-thirty a.m.'

'Is everything all right?' she asked anxiously, straining to see his shape in the darkness. 'You're very late. I was getting worried.'

'The damned car broke down on the way back.'

'Oh, no!' She fumbled for the bedside light, and switched it on. In the golden light, she blinked at him anxiously. 'I *knew* something had gone wrong!'

He was wearing jeans and a sweater, and he looked ravishingly handsome. He smiled. 'Well, I'm enjoying the concern, but luckily it wasn't too far from civilisation. We were able to walk to an inn, and ring for a replacement car from Lerida. It took ages to arrive. That's why we're so late. But there was no real problem. We had dinner and sat by a log fire while we waited.'

Leila pushed the blonde hair away from her eyes. 'Trust you to land on your feet. It sounds rather a nice sort of adventure for the children.'

'It could have been much worse.' His hand had reached out, stroking her face, and she snuggled her cheek into his palm, revelling in his touch.

'I'm so glad you're back,' she murmured.

'Are you?' he replied, sitting on her bed beside her, and caressing her tumbled hair.

'Hmm.' It was so good to feel him close, to feel the loving touch of his hands, to see those beautiful tiger's eyes watching her so intently.

'I would have rung you, but there was no phone at the inn. So I thought I'd see if you were still awake.'

'I'm glad you came. I wasn't sleeping very well at all.'

'Well, I didn't mean to wake you. I just wanted to tell you we were back.'

'Don't go,' she said in a low, urgent voice as he prepared to rise. His eyes met hers, so smokily knowing that she flushed, and struggled for something sensible to say. 'Did you—did you have a nice trip?'

'Awful,' he said succinctly.

'Awful?' She looked at him. 'Why?'

'Three reasons. The first was that Terry missed you, and the second was that Tracey missed you.'

She looked at him from under her lashes. 'You said there were three reasons why your trip was awful, but you've only told me two. What was the third reason?' she asked.

'The third reason...' His voice was husky, his eyes watching her mouth. 'The third reason was me. I've missed you so much, Leila. Missed you until it was an ache. I had to come and see you tonight, I couldn't wait until tomorrow.'

'Oh, Blaize...' She reached for him.

He moved over to take her in his arms, and buried his face against the warm, scented skin of her throat. 'What have you done to me?' he said, his voice slurred against her skin. 'You've enchanted me, you little witch!'

He kissed her, his tongue teasing her lips apart to explore the moist inner secrets of her mouth. She clung to him tightly, feeling the ecstasy of his embrace flood her soul.

She was wearing only a flimsy silk nightie, and, as his caressing hands pushed aside the bedclothes and moved across her body, it was almost as though she were naked to his touch. Their kiss deepened into passion, Leila's fingers plucking at the rough wool jersey he wore, until he broke away from her and stripped it off impatiently.

His naked skin was like hot velvet under her palms, and she claimed his lean, muscular torso with aching hunger.

'I've missed you, too,' she whimpered. 'You've hardly said a word to me all week, hardly looked at me, even. You're so cruel to me!'

'Cruel to myself. I want you.' She barely recognised the strained, rough voice as Blaize's. 'Things have gone so wrong between us, and I want to make them right. I want to make love to you, Leila...'

'Yes,' she whispered, arching to him. Nothing mattered any more, not even that he was committed to marry Katherine Henessey. She wanted his love tonight, wanted something to keep, for the rest of her life, even if she lost him for ever. 'Yes,' she whispered again. 'Love me, Blaize, love me...'

He was kissing her hands, kissing her fingers, her palms, the fluttering pulses that betrayed her wildly beating heart. 'Every inch of you is so beautiful,' he marvelled softly. 'Every detail so perfect...the most perfectly lovely woman I've ever known.'

Leila watched him in melting desire as his slow adoration moved up her arms, across her shoulders, finding the tender places in her neck where the nerves tingled at his touch, whispering the secrets of his need into the sensitive hollows of her ears.

His mouth roamed down her throat and collarbone, seeking her breasts as his fingers fumbled with the buttons of her nightie. She stopped him long enough to strip the garment off, wanting to be naked for him.

A fiery intensity possessed her as he took her in his arms, his kisses moving with consuming hunger across her breasts, teasing her nipples into peaks of desire, tracking down across the plane of her stomach, as though he were intent on fulfilling that promise he had made her long ago—that he would kiss every inch of her body, taste every inch of her skin.

He whispered her name as he trailed kisses along her slender thighs, tasting the silky skin with a tongue that drew erotic patterns on her flesh. Her initial shyness was consumed in the devouring heat of Blaize's hunger for her. Leila arched with the electric pleasure he gave her, her fingers knotting in his thick, crisp hair.

'Touch me,' he commanded unsteadily, his voice rough in his throat. 'Don't you know how I've longed for your touch, my darling?'

Shivering, Leila obeyed, her unskilled fingers tracing the lean, hard contours of his back and flanks. He was so beautiful, like a poured-bronze god come to life. It was marvellous to touch him like this, the pent-up desire of weeks seeming to concentrate itself in her fingertips. Yet she was so ignorant, so unskilled. Her body would not obey the unbounded reach of her imagination.

Terrified that he would think her clumsy and inept, she leaned forward to press her lips to his skin, touching tiny little kisses to his stomach, his lean ribs, the small, hard man's nipples that studded his muscular chest.

His breath was coming faster and shallower, his response to her untaught touch unmistakable. She felt his fingers lacing through the golden hair at her nape, felt his lean body twist in her arms as his nerve-endings responded to her butterfly-light caresses.

She fumbled inexpertly with the button on his jeans, pressing kisses against Blaize's hard, flat stomach, and heard his long-drawn shudder of passion. In the taut silence, the zip of his jeans was a ripping sound that was almost unnaturally loud. Her tremulous fingers explored his thighs, longing for the purpose and experience necessary to excite so expert a lover as Blaize.

She traced the outline of his body with tremblingly delicate fingers, searching for the places that would give him most pleasure. She knew so little of a man's anatomy, was so hampered by her shyness...

'You're tormenting me,' he whispered, arching towards her as though unable to contain the desire he felt. Leila pressed her face against him, burying her mouth in the dark hair that shadowed his manhood, feeling the heat of his arousal searing her cheek. Blaize's fingers bit into her shoulders, drawing her away, unable to bear her contact.

'Don't do this to me,' he implored, his green eyes dark with desire. 'Your touch is so delicate that it maddens me!'

'I—I don't know what to do,' she said, her throat constricted. 'I'm so sorry...'

'Sorry?' His mouth sought the swollen curves of her breasts. 'Sorry about what?'

'You're the first,' she told him in a shaky voice, cradling his head in her arms. 'You're the only one, Blaize.'

His kiss was tender, adoring. 'Are you telling me you're a virgin?'

'Yes...'

'Leila...' He paused, watching her face intently in the soft light. 'Why didn't you tell me that weeks ago?'

'It's not something I could just blurt out...are you going to mock me?'

'My darling!' He laughed softly. 'Mock you? When you hold my heart and soul in your hands? But you've nonplussed me, my love. I've never been in bed with a virgin before.'

'Don't you know what to do?' she teased huskily, as though gaining courage from his tender words. 'Then you'd better let me find my own way...'

This time, she was bolder, surer. She taught herself about him, her fingers finding their own way to his desire, her lips following to trail slow, sensuous kisses down his loins, until Blaize's breathing was harsh and uneven, broken with repeated whispers of her name that sounded almost like a prayer.

When he could bear it no longer, he rolled away from her, and then it was his turn to explore, to caress, to teach her the pleasure that lay in her skin, her flesh, within the miraculous design of her woman's body.

'I want you never to forget tonight,' he whispered, adoring her body with his mouth and fingers. 'I want it to last forever...'

He seemed lost with wonder at the arc of her hips under the smooth flesh, the golden down that tracked almost invisibly across her skin. She gasped as his tongue traced the lacy scallops of her briefs, a deliberately teasing torment that mimicked her own uncertain caresses, yet did so with a wicked expertise that was almost cruel. She wanted to beg him not to make her wait, yet the waiting was so sweet that the words died in her throat.

Blaize's kiss slowly became shamelessly erotic, the teasing graduating into fulfilment as his mouth found the melting centre of her need, transcending any shyness that might have lingered. Leila moaned, hunger peaking unbearably in her, the tautness of her body telling him how much she needed him.

There was no fear as he moved over her to possess her, only an expectation, a sense of wonder. Where his tongue had been almost unbearably gentle, his man's body was hard and thrusting, a possessive mastery that made her gasp briefly at the short, sharp pain that made her a woman.

And then Leila was lost in the slow, expanding dialogue between their bodies, his arms crushing her to him, the fierce heat that became pleasure, and then ecstasy. Her whole being was caught up in the coming together of their souls, the union that grew and intensified with the majesty of a rising sun, with the detail of a drop of dew swelling at the edge of a rose-petal, growing too heavy to hold itself, bursting into a glittering new world that only contained two people, Blaize and Leila, who cried and whispered in one another's arms, who could not find words enough to describe the love they had found, the love they had made...

The majesty of a rising sun.

Her room was flooded with crimson and gold as she opened her eyes, her mind still blank from the drugged sleep of satiety. Her whole body was tingling with pleasure, as though Blaize had left some chemical in her veins, some factor that continued to pleasure her, long after the event.

'I'm so very sorry, my love.'

She rolled sleepily to face him. He was smiling as he put the breakfast-tray down beside her. 'I know you should be left to sleep undisturbed, and six o'clock is an ungodly hour for anyone to wake, let alone someone who spent most of the night making passionate love...'

He kissed her smiling mouth, then the pink rosebuds of her naked nipples.

'Is it really six o'clock?' she murmured.

'Hmm.' His interest in her breasts was showing every danger of spreading to other areas of her body, but he stopped himself with an obvious effort. 'I wanted us to have breakfast together,' he explained, pouring the coffee for them both, and sitting beside her. 'And I don't want our night of passion getting all round the house. Not just yet, anyway.'

The black stubble that etched his face somehow made him all the more devastatingly male, and she reached up to touch his cheek, then slid her hands possessively under his dark blue dressing-gown to touch the hard, muscular body that had loved her so comprehensively last night.

'What's going to become of us?' she asked, her troubled mouth quivering as she looked up at him.

'Milk, no sugar, just the way you like it,' he said, and smiled as he passed her a cup of coffee. 'Are you concerned?'

'Yes, Blaize.' She took the cup, and stared down into it. 'You know that I love you, don't you?' she said in a quiet voice.

'You gave me the proof, last night. Vanessa wasn't a virgin, Leila. None of the women I've been with has ever been a virgin. You're the first woman who has given herself to me so completely...'

'But you're going to marry Katherine,' Leila said unsteadily, her eyes blurring.

'Katherine?' He shook his head slightly. 'How could I ever marry a woman I don't love, Leila?'

She almost gasped aloud, and put down her coffee-cup for fear she would spill it. 'Don't you love her?'

'I've never loved her.' His eyes were telling her the truth. 'She was so good with the children, and they seemed so fond of her. I was considering it for their sake, but now I know just how wrong I've been. I've been awake a long time this morning, wondering how I could ever have contemplated marrying a woman who doesn't know me, whom I could never tell all the secrets of my life. I've been wondering how I could have considered marrying Katherine, when real love was waiting for me all the time—real love in the form of a little spitfire called Leila Thomas...'

Now she did gasp, burying her face against his broad chest to stifle the tears. Blaize crushed her close, his arms so strong, so possessive.

'It took that weekend away from you to sort my thoughts out, Leila. We were so damned miserable, all three of us. You must have cast some kind of spell over my children, Leila, as well as over me. I've never seen them pine for anybody like this before. I've been re-

alising how insane I was to think you would ever hurt
either of them.'

Leila drew back to look up at him with adoring eyes.
'Well, whatever you may have thought of me in the past,'
she said awkwardly, 'I really do care about Tracey and
Terry. I didn't mean to upset Tracey on Sunday night.
I can't think what made her cry like that, and I've been
feeling utterly wretched about it all week. If only I could
have spoken to her, asked her what had happened...'
She met his eyes. 'I was only trying to help. Maybe it's
some kind of frustrated maternal instinct. When a
woman without a child sees a child without a mother,
you see, it sometimes goes to her head a little.'

Blaize stared at her hard for a moment. 'I appreciate
that,' he said at last, his voice sounding rusty. 'I was
way out of line last Sunday, I know that now, but Tracey
was in a real state... I once said that you've got something I don't have,' he went on. 'Whatever that something is, it's enabled you to get through to my daughter.
You're the only person who's been able to do that in the
past few years. Come to that, you're the only person
who's ever been able to get through to *me*, full stop.'
He touched her cheek. 'There's something that's been
haunting me, Leila. It's your conviction that I have so
many affairs on the side. You even said that Tracey had
told you it was true. I thought you were lying, then. But
I don't any more. I know now that you're incapable of
falsehood.'

'Tracey did tell me that.' Leila nodded, her eyes wide
in her pale, oval face. 'There's something else, Blaize,
something you don't know. Tracey came to meet me at
the airport. Alone. She drove all the way in your car.'

'You're dreaming. Or I am!'

'Neither of us is dreaming, I swear it.'

His mouth was open, as though the words had stuck in his throat. 'For pity's sake,' he said at last, sounding shaken. 'You'd better tell me everything!'

She told him what had happened, giving him a full account of Tracey's arrival at the airport, of what the girl had said to her, and of their talk in the motorway service station.

She saw the blood drain from his cheeks as she spoke, and knew that this was hitting him hard. When she'd finished, he sat in silence. The muscles along his jaw were clenched tight, and his eyes stared into space, as though he were searching for some kind of inner answer.

Leila waited in an unhappy silence, wondering whether there was going to be another storm. Whether this time she really *would* be on her way to London, her life shattered.

When he looked at her, his eyes were dark. 'Something is very wrong here,' he said at last. 'It's been wrong ever since Katherine Henessey came into my life, and I'm going to set it right today, for the first and last time. But, before I do, Leila, I want you to know that I'm not, and never have been, a womaniser. All those affairs Tracey told you about—they're pure fantasy. Do you believe me?'

'Yes,' she said simply. 'I believe you, Blaize.'

He glanced at this watch. 'It's six-thirty. Let's go and see Tracey, now.'

Was it because the day had started so early that it had seemed so long? Or was it because it had been filled with so much emotion, some of it sad, but most of it beautiful?

Or just because it was the first day of her new life, a life that had Blaize as its centre?

They walked through the garden in the twilight, arms wrapped tightly around one another. The setting sun gilded the leaves of the roses, turning the surface of the pool into molten bronze, rippling silver where the two children splashed and frolicked.

'I can still hardly believe it,' Blaize said, shaking his head. 'That a woman like Katherine could play on the feelings of a defenceless child like that, a child she claimed to love...'

'It wasn't Tracey she loved,' Leila said gently. 'It was you. And love makes people do terrible things, Blaize. More terrible than hate, sometimes.'

'Love?' He looked at her, the tiger's eyes now gentle and adoring. 'No, Leila. Love is what you have in your heart. Katherine has never known love, and I doubt whether she ever will.'

It had come as a horrible shock to learn, from a sobbing Tracey, just how Katherine Henessey had been manipulating her emotions over the past months. Having gained Tracey's trust and affection, she had proceeded to use her influence to try and exert pressure over Blaize, guessing that Blaize would only ever consider marriage with a woman who really cared about his children. With Tracey on her side, Katherine had thought she could not fail in her quest of becoming the second Mrs Oliver.

But the influence she had exerted had grown more ruthless, less sincere, as her goal drew closer. It had been her insecurity that had made her convince Tracey that every woman who came near her father was somehow either having an affair with him, or in imminent danger of having an affair with him.

'I'll never forgive her for that,' Blaize said harshly. 'Thank heaven Terry was too young to have been caught up in her wiles. But to tell a fifteen-year-old girl that her father can't keep his hands off other women...she deserves to be shot for that.'

Katherine might have preferred being shot, Leila thought with a wince, remembering Blaize's face as he'd driven off to see Katherine earlier today. Blaize had been a very angry man. He hadn't told her what he'd said to Katherine when he'd returned two hours later, but she knew that it would have been worse than the clean impact of a bullet.

He had told her, however, that Katherine had broken down and confessed everything. How she had tried to enlist Tracey's help against any woman who appeared to pose a threat, or become a rival, for Blaize's attention. How it had been through her urging that Tracey had been driven to the dangerous and foolish lengths of driving to the airport to meet Leila.

That had puzzled Leila, until Blaize had shown her the letter that Carol Clarewell had sent Blaize, extolling the virtues of a young secretary called Leila Thomas, whom she was sending out to Spain for a six-week spell...

'She does make me sound rather a paragon of virtues,' Leila said awkwardly, flushing as she read the eulogy Carol had written. 'You would think I was some kind of superwoman.'

'You would think right,' Blaize had nodded. 'Reading that letter now, it's easy to see how it could have disturbed Katherine to the point of mounting an anti-Leila campaign before you'd even arrived.'

Tracey had confirmed it all. Through her tears, she'd explained how Katherine had worked her up until her own longing for a stable marriage for her father had driven her into the madness and hostility of risking her life on that long, long drive to the airport.

And it had, of course, been Katherine who had upset her so badly on Sunday night. When she'd learned that Leila had been trying to help the girl, she had launched a fierce attack on Tracey, accusing her of disloyalty to herself, and doing her best to nullify all of Leila's advice.

Tracey, torn between her loyalties, had been driven to near-hysterics.

Blaize had explained to Tracey, very gently, that all Katherine's lies had been false, that he hadn't been having affairs with any of the women in their lives, and the radiant happiness in Tracey's eyes had been all the evidence he'd needed that she accepted he was telling the truth.

And the tears of pain had turned into joy as Leila had embraced her, and spoken to her in a gentle voice.

'Katherine won't ever bother you again, Tracey. I want to tell you something. Your father has asked me to be his wife, and I've said yes. I know you already have a mother, so I won't say that I want to take her place. But I do want to be your friend, yours and Terry's, for all my life. You make me very happy, and I want to do the same for you.'

There had been no doubt about the children's approval, no more than there had been about her own joy.

Her happiness was seamless, flawless, a golden light that filled her, just as this sunset was filling the universe around them now.

'Children are resilient,' she said to Blaize, listening to the happy shrieks of Terry and Tracey as they played together in the pool. 'Do they look as though they've taken any serious harm, either of them?'

'No,' Blaize admitted with a smile. 'I've never seen them so happy.'

'Tracey will have forgotten about Katherine in a week,' Leila assured him. 'So will we. And we'll never give either of them anything but happiness and security, as long as we live, Blaize. I swear it.'

'I know they adore you,' Blaize said, drawing her close. 'That much is obvious from the way they've behaved today. But how do you think they will take to having new brothers and sisters in a couple of years?'

'You and I both have known what loneliness is,' she said softly, looking into his eyes. 'It's a lesson that has taught us how to surround ourselves with happiness. I think that all our children will be happy and healthy and wise, Blaize. And maybe, in time, we can share some of our own happiness with all the members of our families—even the ones who are outside its limits now...'

'You've helped me to crystallise a lot of things.' Blaize nodded. 'For a long time, I've been thinking of freeing myself from some of the burdens of my work. Now I'm going to do it, Leila. When we get back to England, I'm going to rearrange a lot of things. I want time, lots of time, oceans of time to love you in.'

'And your children.'

'And the children you and I will make.' He smiled. 'I love you,' he said, his mouth closing her eyelids.

'Ah,' she said with a little shudder of pleasure. 'That's the first time you've ever said that to me.'

'Did it sound rusty? I'm not in the habit of saying those three little words.'

'You'd better get some practice, then,' she invited huskily.

'I love you,' he said again, crushing her. 'I love you, Leila, only you, forever... if only I could be sure that I could hold your interest for the rest of our lives!'

'Hold my interest?' she echoed. 'You're my life, Blaize. I enjoyed working, but I've discovered that I want more. I want your love. I want a family, I want the fulfilment that only you can give me.'

'You won't pine for the excitement of your job?' he asked.

She touched his lips, almost amused at his lack of self-confidence, when her love for him went so very deep. 'I shall pine for nothing, Blaize. I never wanted commitment. It frightened me, in fact, but not any more. Now I can't wait to be your wife, and to start our lives together. You are my everything. *I'm* the one who should worry about holding *your* interest!'

'My interest has never been held more securely, or more intensely.' He grinned. 'I once thought I only had one reason for marrying again. But I've just discovered a far more important one—to make sure that I get what you gave me last night, every night, until we're too old to do more than hold hands!'

'Do I really mean that much to you?'

He purred. 'Let me prove it to you...'

'Perhaps we should go and kiss each other somewhere else,' she said shakily, after a long while. 'The children will see us.'

'The children have already seen us,' Blaize said gently, caressing the golden mop of her hair. 'They need to see us. They need the love you can give them, the love that you can't help shedding all around you, like an angel...my angel.'

'Then kiss me again.' Leila smiled, arching her throat to look up at the man she loved. 'And don't stop until I tell you.'